P

"My name's Clint Adams."

"And I'm Kira Vellejo, but I suppose you already knew that."

"Yeah. I did. Things tend to go a little smoother once folks introduce themselves, that's all."

"How very civil of you. Maybe now you can put that gun away."

Clint shook his head. "Besides your name, I also know you're a dangerous woman. I want you to take this," he said while grabbing some rope hanging from his saddle and tossing it to her. "Tie a knot around your ankles and then I'll put the gun away."

Kira bent at the knees to pick up the rope. When she looked up at him, Clint could see the trouble brewing in her eyes. Even with that bit of warning, he wasn't fully prepared for what came next.

She charged him like an angry bull, completely ignoring the pistol in his hand . . .

THE GUNSMITH

295

KIRA'S BOUNTY

J. R. ROBERTS

J

JOVE BOOKS, NEW YORK

THE BERKLEY PUBLISHING GROUP
Published by the Penguin Group
Penguin Group (USA) Inc.
375 Hudson Street, New York, New York 10014, USA
Penguin Group (Canada), 90 Eglinton Avenue East, Suite 700, Toronto, Ontario M4P 2Y3, Canada
(a division of Pearson Penguin Canada Inc.)
Penguin Books Ltd., 80 Strand, London WC2R 0RL, England
Penguin Group Ireland, 25 St. Stephen's Green, Dublin 2, Ireland (a division of Penguin Books Ltd.)
Penguin Group (Australia), 250 Camberwell Road, Camberwell, Victoria 3124, Australia
(a division of Pearson Australia Group Pty. Ltd.)
Penguin Books India Pvt. Ltd., 11 Community Centre, Panchsheel Park, New Delhi—110 017, India
Penguin Group (NZ), Cnr. Airborne and Rosedale Roads, Albany, Auckland 1310, New Zealand
(a division of Pearson New Zealand Ltd.)
Penguin Books (South Africa) (Pty.) Ltd., 24 Sturdee Avenue, Rosebank, Johannesburg 2196,
South Africa

Penguin Books Ltd., Registered Offices: 80 Strand, London WC2R 0RL, England

This is a work of fiction. Names, characters, places, and incidents either are the product of the author's imagination or are used fictitiously, and any resemblance to actual persons, living or dead, business establishments, events, or locales is entirely coincidental.

KIRA'S BOUNTY

A Jove Book / published by arrangement with the author

PRINTING HISTORY
Jove edition / July 2006

ISBN: 0-515-14158-5

JOVE®
Jove Books are published by The Berkley Publishing Group,
a division of Penguin Group (USA) Inc.,
375 Hudson Street, New York, New York 10014.
JOVE is a registered trademark of Penguin Group (USA) Inc.
The "J" design is a trademark belonging to Penguin Group (USA) Inc.

PRINTED IN THE UNITED STATES OF AMERICA

10 9 8 7 6 5 4 3 2 1

ONE

The desert wind felt like a grinding wheel against Marshal Vicker's face. It was a dry, constant movement of grit through the air that rattled noisily against windowpanes and collected in every nook and cranny of the crooked boardwalk. Even for a town that was stuck in the middle of the Nevada desert, the wind was getting tough to bear. In fact, Marshal Vicker was the only man in sight on any of Taloosa's streets.

But the little whirlwinds that were kicked up here and there weren't the only signs of life in Taloosa. Even if the locals weren't quick to stroll outside if they had a choice, they weren't about to keep quiet just on account of a nasty wind. Taloosa was the sort of place that was used to bracing itself against days like this, much like a turtle was used to pulling its head into its shell.

Some places tended to do better business when the winds kicked up like this. Those places were the Armadillo Saloon and Miss Pryde's Varieties, both of which were within half a block of each other. Marshal Vicker was leaning against a post between those two spots with his duster buttoned up to the neck and his bandanna fitted over his nose and mouth. His hands were tucked into his pockets,

1

one hand reaching all the way through to the .45-caliber revolver holstered at his hip.

As the wind gusted to a powerful roar and the gritty mess swirled in front of him, Vicker's only reaction was to narrow his squint just a bit more and tuck his chin a little closer to his chest. The edges of his coat flapped against his legs and the post, but the rest of him didn't even budge.

Before too long, it seemed as though the wind simply ran out of breath and gave up in trying to move him. When it died down again, Vicker lifted his chin and took a quick glance around. He spotted the pair of riders heading into town almost immediately.

One of them sat upon a big, dark horse. The other rode on what appeared to be a dun. Vicker had a good eye for horseflesh and could have picked out a lot more about the animals, but he was more interested in their riders.

Desert towns like Taloosa saw more than their share of bad men, simply because they were stuck out in the middle of nowhere and all but forgotten by the civilized world. Marshal Vicker discouraged that kind of thinking whenever he could. In those instances, the .45 at his hip did most of the talking.

He'd worn his badge long enough to spot trouble, but it was too early for any man to say if these two posed any sort of threat. Still, most men who knew the desert had better places to hide in the middle of a storm than right in the middle of it. Bad men liked to come into town during winds like these. That way, they could come and go without being seen.

Taloosa's bank had been robbed three times in storms like these by men who'd camped outside of town, waiting for the wind to pick up like this. Killers had escaped into the elements and were never seen again. Wanted men broke out of Vicker's own jail and only needed to run twenty yards before they disappeared.

That was why Vicker tended to wrap himself up and

stand watch when the winds kicked up and howled like they did right now. His jail was empty, and he didn't have anything else to do but make sure it stayed that way. Sometimes, one vigilant soul was enough to make a bad man think twice about stirring up whatever trouble he had in mind.

Marshal Vicker intended on being that man.

That was his job.

He knew plenty well that most bad men would head straight for their business as soon as they got in town. Now was the time for a robber to rob or a killer to strike. Since these two riders didn't seem to be in too much of a hurry, Vicker was able to satisfy himself that they weren't out to rob anyone.

Any robber worth his salt would have steered toward the bank or some other target rather than waste the element of surprise by riding straight into town. By the looks of it, they were headed for the Armadillo or Miss Pryde's.

Beneath his coat, his fingers wrapped around the grip of his .45 and settled over its trigger. He kept the gun holstered, but lifted it just enough so he could clear leather and shoot through his duster in the blink of an eye.

Thinking about that, Vicker winced.

He used his free hand to pull open his duster so it flapped freely against his chest.

No need to ruin a good coat.

TWO

Lillian was an ample girl, but had everything in all the right places. And in some places, she had it twice. That was the reason she could charge by the half hour or hour instead of for each time she rolled in the sheets with her customers. Lillian was the sort of girl that a man wanted to take his time with, and they were always willing to pay handsomely for the privilege.

At the moment, Lillian was in her own room at Miss Pryde's, which was one of the fancier ones there. Her long, dark hair was splayed out over the pillows stacked under her head and she closed her eyes as if to display the painted lids. She didn't need any rouge on her cheeks to give them color, however. The vigorous movements of her body and quick breathing were flushing her cheeks well enough.

"That's it, baby," she said while wrapping her arms around the man on top of her. "Just like that."

Lillian's skin was lightly tanned and as smooth as the most expensive imported creams could get it. In fact, the man on top of her could barely tell where her skin stopped and the occasional bits of silk began. The wispy nightgown she'd been wearing was hanging off one shoulder and bunched around her waist. Like most of Lillian's customers, this man wasn't patient enough to peel it all the way off her.

"Goddamn," the man grunted. "You're worth every dollar I paid for ya."

She nodded and shifted beneath him, adjusting one foot against the mattress while she rubbed the other leg along the small of his back. "You've still got plenty of time, baby. I want you to make good use of every minute."

"Oh, I will," he replied, even though his breaths were already starting to come in quick bursts. "You can . . . bet on . . . that."

Although she enjoyed the feel of the man thrusting between her legs, Lillian slowly closed her arms around him to slow him down. Before he could get too upset about being pulled from his rhythm, Lillian was easing herself out from beneath him.

Smiling easily and tugging the nightgown over her ample curves, Lillian crawled to the edge of the bed and perched there like a cat. "You look so good. How about I take a ride for myself?"

The frustration that had cropped up on the man's face was quickly replaced by fresh excitement. "That's somethin' I ain't never tried before," he gasped.

And that didn't shock Lillian in the slightest.

"Really?" she asked with a surprised look on her face as she pushed him down and climbed on top of him. "I would think a stud like you would know every way under the sun to please a woman."

"Oh, I know plenty. Fact is I . . ." His words trailed off into a prolonged breath as Lillian took hold of his rigid cock and guided it to the soft thatch of hair between her legs.

Her pussy was soft in every way imaginable. The downy hair tickled his skin as he slid inside her. The smooth, wet lips wrapped around his penis and took him all the way inside. As she eased down onto him, Lillian wore a smile of her own. It was that genuine smile that allowed her to charge as much as she did.

While most working girls found a way to tolerate or fool the men they took to their beds, Lillian truly seemed to enjoy what she did. When a man like Earl actually sat back and let her do some of the work for a change, she actually did enjoy it.

Lillian's large breasts hung well within reach as she settled in and rocked back and forth. When Earl reached up to grab them, Lillian purred contentedly and stayed right where she was. "That's nice, baby," she said. "You've got good hands."

If Earl said something after that, Lillian didn't hear it. Instead, she was too busy riding up and down on his cock until she found just the right way to put that smile on her face. At first, she was using her hips to rock back and forth while gliding along the length of his erection. Then, Lillian got more of her legs beneath her until she was supporting most of her weight using all of her legs.

Once she was crouching down and squatting on him, she pressed her hands firmly against Earl's chest and began bouncing up and down even faster. Lillian tossed her hair back over one shoulder and curled her lips into a lavish smile. Her eyes remained closed as she rode Earl's cock faster and faster.

From where he was, Earl figured he had one of the best views in creation. Stretched out on his back, his hands resting upon Lillian's generous hips, he let his eyes drift over her ample curves as if he was merely enjoying a vivid dream.

Lillian's nightgown was draped over her thighs and was gathered up behind her to brush against Earl's knees. The straps holding up the top of the nightgown were off both shoulders, allowing her large breasts to sway freely. Her nipples were hard and sensitive against Earl's palms. Soon, sweat from her body made the silk cling to her flesh like a second skin. The moisture between her legs was dripping down the length of Earl's cock.

Since she'd started bouncing on top of him, Lillian hadn't heard Earl make so much as a peep. When she looked down at him, she saw him staring up at her with wide eyes and a nervous smile. Suddenly, she could feel him start to thrust up eagerly into her.

After one pump of his hips, he started pounding into her again and again in a quickening pace. Although she liked the feel of him driving up into her wide-open legs, she patted him on the chest and said, "Best watch yourself now."

"I'm done watchin'," Earl grunted as he grabbed hold of Lillian's hips and kept pounding. "I can see you like that!"

Lillian eased herself onto her knees and lowered herself so her breasts were pressed against his chest. "Still plenty of time, baby."

But Earl wasn't listening to a word she said. His eyes were clenched shut and his face was twisted into the determined expression of a man who was in the firm grip of his impulses. One of his arms wrapped around Lillian's back while his other hand clamped onto her backside. She let out a pleased little moan when she felt him slap her rump a bit, which added even more fuel to Earl's fire.

Since it was useless to try and slow the man down, Lillian enjoyed the ride for as long as it lasted. Unfortunately, she could tell that it wasn't going to last much longer.

She did her best to slow him down by settling on top of him and keeping her own body steady, but Lillian wasn't a miracle worker. Earl's eyes were fixed upon her swaying breasts, and he pumped his cock into the warm wetness of Lillian's body.

Even the sweet smell of her hair brushing against his face was enough to excite him further, until he finally gave one more powerful thrust.

Lillian felt him explode inside her, but kept grinding her

hips to her own rhythm. Propping herself up using both arms, she kept riding him until she could feel the start of her own set of shivers beneath her skin. She moved one hand across her breasts while using the other to draw quick little circles around her clitoris.

Closing her eyes and moving her hips, Lillian started to feel her own climax approaching. As long as she kept her hand busy while moving against Earl's body, she might just—

"Get off'a me, woman," Earl grunted. "I need to get somethin' to drink."

Oh, well, she thought while rolling to one side. At least he'd paid in advance.

THREE

Marshal Vicker planted his feet upon the boardwalk one shoulder width apart. He stuck out one hand to the approaching riders while keeping the other stuffed into his ripped pocket and wrapped around his .45.

At first, it seemed as though the riders hadn't seen him. Then, the larger of the two turned a pair of sharp, narrowed eyes in his direction. That one reached out to tap the other's arm while bringing his horse to a stop.

Both riders were covered in so much dust and sand that Vicker couldn't even be certain of the color of their clothes. They looked more like lizards that had slithered out from under a rock, since their bodies had one solid shape that was broken only by the occasional wrinkle. Their bandannas were matted right onto their faces, completing the reptilian appearance.

"Where are you men headed?" Vicker asked.

The bigger man's head shifted slightly, which sent a trickle of sand from where it had collected at his neck.

Now that he was close enough, Vicker could see the weapons the riders were carrying. Although he could only see the pistol butt just beneath the smaller one's coat, it was easy enough to spot the holster around the bigger one's waist as well as the rifle slung onto the side of his saddle.

"What was that?" the bigger one asked. His voice was muffled through his dirty bandanna, and sounded almost like a snarl drifting through the swirling winds.

"I asked where you men were headed," Vicker repeated.

"Out of the storm for one."

Leaning forward, the smaller man added, "I got a friend a few streets down." When he spoke, sand poured off the brim of his hat like water flowing over the lip of a rock wall. "He owns a saloon called the Vegas Pearl."

"Ain't no place like that around here," Vicker said. "Ain't never been a place like that."

"Sure there is. The Vegas Pearl!" When he saw that repeating the name didn't cause the enlightenment he was after, the smaller rider looked over to the bigger one. Looking away from the hard stare coming at him from the other rider, the smaller fellow grudgingly asked, "This is Las Vegas, ain't it?"

Vicker stared at both men for a few solid moments. Once he could see that neither man was going for his weapon and that they were both dead serious, he broke out in a laugh that shook free a good amount of the dust that had settled into every fold of his coat.

"You're close to a day's ride from Las Vegas," Vicker said.

The bigger rider shook his head. When he let out an exasperated breath, it formed a slight bubble in the bandanna.

Having spent the last few minutes preparing himself for the worst where the two riders were concerned, Vicker found himself feeling more than relieved once he realized that the men weren't just more dirt blown in from the storm. In fact, seeing the aggravation in the bigger one's eyes, he actually felt bad for stomping up to them with his hand on his gun.

"How long you two been riding?" Vicker asked.

Glad to look away from the smaller man, the bigger rider replied, "Almost a day. Apparently, it's been in the wrong direction."

"A storm like this'd mix up the best of them. Come on this way and get yer bearings."

When the horses saw they were headed for an open stable door, they practically ran for it without being told. Those doors turned out to be nearly as wide as the shack they were attached to, and they rattled on their hinges with every howl of the wind.

The structure was less than half the size of a normal barn and only had a few overhead bins instead of a loft. Still, it could hold four horses and was only half full, which made it a very welcome sight for several very sore eyes.

Both riders had to dismount quickly before they were knocked from their saddles by one of the shack's low beams. The moment their boots hit the ground, they batted at their shoulders and took off their hats to smack them against their knees. This was enough to cause a swirl of dust within the shack that almost rivaled the storm outside.

"Jesus, Ben," the bigger rider said. "I told you a dozen times we were headed in the wrong direction, but you were too pigheaded to listen."

Benjamin Cable looked a bit taller now that he wasn't in the saddle. He stood up a little straighter and carried himself somewhat differently, which accounted for the difference. He was a wiry fellow with what appeared to be black hair underneath the layers of grit that had made it under his hat. When he pulled down the bandanna, he revealed a youthful face that was smeared with dust and sweat.

"Well, excuse the hell out of me," Ben grunted as he stripped the saddle from his horse without even needing to look at what he was doing. "I did my damn'dest to get here and I think the fact that I got us to shelter at all is testimony to my skill as a guide."

The bigger man still had his bandanna over his face as

he stared at Ben. Shaking his head, he pulled the bandanna off and used it to wipe away some of the grime from his cheeks and forehead. "That cave I found was big enough to shelter us and the horses for the whole storm. I even had plenty of bacon to cook until you managed to drop it somewhere along the way."

"If you two want to discuss this over some whiskey, the Armadillo is across the street and to the left," Vicker said. "Miss Pryde's serves a damn fine steak as well as . . . other comforts."

"You mean women?" Ben asked as his ears perked up.

Vicker was already headed out the door. "Yeah. That's what I mean."

Before the marshal could leave, he felt a tap on his shoulder. When he turned around, he saw the bigger man extending a hand.

"We appreciate the welcome."

Vicker nodded and shook the man's hand. Before he could say another word, his own ears perked up at the sound of gunshots mixed in amid the howling wind. "I'd better get going."

FOUR

Ben flinched when he heard the large door slam shut. His hand had already dropped toward his pistol when he looked over to the other man beside him. "Damn, Clint, were those gunshots?"

Clint quickly pulled the buckles loose and removed the saddle from Eclipse's back. He took off the filthy blanket underneath as well and brushed out some of the dust matted in the Darley Arabian's mane. "Yeah," he replied. "Those were gunshots."

"You think they came from some of those banditos we were hunting down?"

Tossing a glare in Ben's direction, Clint asked, "You mean those banditos that were riding to Las Vegas?"

After a few shifts of his feet, Ben said, "Maybe them . . . or maybe some of them others. There were others, you know."

"I know, but I doubt it was them."

"It could be them."

Clint drew his modified Colt and turned it on its side. While rolling the cylinder using the palm of his free hand, he blew as much of the dust from the moving parts as he could. Once he was satisfied that the gun would work if it was needed, he dropped it back into its holster. Only then did he look back to Ben and say, "Could be, but I doubt it is."

Before Ben could put up another argument, he saw Clint push the door open and head outside. He followed, mostly out of habit than anything else. "We've been riding together for a while now."

"It's only been a few weeks."

"But we've been through some tough spots."

"Most of those were your fault."

"And we pulled each other through them spots because we work good together," Ben continued, completely ignoring Clint's grumbled replies. "As your partner, I say we should get something to eat and let this town's law handle whatever is out there. If it's not one of the men we were after, then why bother?"

"This town's got a lawman. He was the one who showed us to this place. And since you weren't able to spot the badge under his coat," Clint added with a smirk, "I don't think I'll trust your instincts over my own."

Clint stepped into the storm and quickly tied the bandanna back around his face. Although it took a moment to steel himself against the gritty winds, he quickly fell into the same steps and breathing patterns that had gotten him through the desert and into this town in the first place. Even through the winds, he could hear Ben stomping up alongside him.

"I'm thirsty, Clint! And hungry! We don't even know if there's any money to be made in this!"

"Then meet me over at that saloon. I can see it right over there. I'll be along as soon as I check in on those shots."

"Why the hell even bother, though?"

Clint's only answer to that was a shrug as he pulled his hat down tighter and shouldered his way through the moving wall of dust and sand. The edges of all the buildings were lost amid the filthy winds, but the lighted windows and dark boards of the walkways could be picked out in the middle of it all. Clint was headed toward a large building on the corner. The dark outline of Marshal Vicker was just approaching that building's front door.

Ben paused for a moment as if he was going to watch both of the other men walk away. His eyes brightened a bit when he saw the sign on that building marking it as Miss Pryde's Varieties. "Aw, hell," Ben grumbled into his bandanna. "I was gonna get a steak anyways."

Marshal Vicker stepped up to the front door of Miss Pryde's and reached out for the handle. He stopped with his arm extended, then dropped it down to cover the grip of his pistol as he turned on the balls of his feet to face whoever was coming up behind him. His scowling eyes quickly found Clint standing there with both hands raised.

"What the hell are you doing sneaking up on me like that?" Vicker asked.

"I heard the shots and thought I could lend a hand."

"I don't need any helpers."

Clint glanced to the left and right before saying, "I don't see any deputies coming to your side."

Although Vicker relaxed a bit, he still kept his hand close to his gun. "No need for you to mix up in whatever this is."

"And there was no need for you to pull me and my friend in out of that storm. Besides, this is probably just some scuffle. Having someone along for appearances might help calm some horny cowboy down a little quicker."

Once again, Vicker smiled. "You work as a lawman before?"

"I've had some experience."

"What about your friend?"

Clint looked around just in time to see Ben rush up the steps leading to the front door. "He can handle himself well enough."

Vicker nodded and let a grim, no-nonsense expression cover his face. He then turned and pushed the door open and stomped into Miss Pryde's. "What the hell's going on in here?" he bellowed.

As expected, most of the people in the immediate vicinity were women in various stages of undress. Some wore fancy dresses, complete with pearls and formal gloves. Others wore frilly underclothes that didn't leave much to the imagination. A few of the girls scampering into another room were only wearing their formal gloves.

All of them were scared.

One of the women stepped forward. She was an attractive blonde in her late forties dressed in a simple, yet elegant dress. "Marshal, thank God you're here."

"Did I hear a shot coming from in here, Claudia?"

The blonde nodded and grabbed Vicker's hand so she could pull him toward a wide staircase. "It came from upstairs. There was some yelling and few things were tossed around. After that, there was a shot."

"Since then?"

"It's been quiet," Claudia replied with a worried expression on her face.

Vicker had that same expression on his face as he craned his neck to look up the stairs. "You know which room it came from?"

"Lillian's."

Vicker didn't need any more instructions than that. He drew his pistol and nodded toward some of the other girls gathered nearby. "Get everyone away from these stairs and the front door. If some asshole wants to bolt outta here, I don't want anyone getting in his way."

Claudia nodded and shifted her eyes toward the two men flanking Vicker. "Who are they?"

"Concerned citizens," Vicker replied. "Now clear these girls out like I asked."

"All right." Moving through the room, Claudia swept up the frightened ladies and corralled them into what appeared to be a dining room. After giving Vicker one more grateful nod, she closed the door.

"You men still want in on this?" the marshal asked.

"Beats being lost in a dust storm," Clint replied as he walked up the stairs behind Vicker.

Grudgingly, Ben drew his own pistol and brought up the rear. "To hell with you, Adams," he grumbled.

Miss Pryde's Varieties was more like a nice hotel than a whore house. The floors were either polished hardwood or covered in elegant carpets. Every bit of furniture was well tended and adorned with subtle feminine touches. The doors upstairs were even numbered the way every hotel's rooms were numbered, but it was the smell that tipped the place's hand.

No hotel smelled as good as Miss Pryde's Varieties. There was a hint of perfume wafting on every breath Clint took. Judging by the look of the ladies that had been downstairs, Miss Pryde's was the sort of place that got high marks in every area. Even the scents of food coming from that dining room had set Clint's stomach to growling.

Compared to the storm that they'd only recently escaped, the place was only a step or two beneath the Promised Land. The wide smile plastered across Ben's face showed that he was thinking the same thing.

Those pleasant thoughts were flushed straight out of Clint and Ben's minds when they heard the thump and shatter coming from one of the rooms further down the hall. Marshal Vicker didn't even flinch, and headed straight for one door in particular.

". . . cking *bitch*!" came a man's voice from the other side of that door.

That was followed by yet another thump as something was tossed against the door.

Vicker stood away from the door and reached out to rap his knuckles against it. Before he could even announce who he was, a bullet punched through the door and hissed within inches of his face.

Flinching slightly, Vicker said, "I'd say this is the place."

FIVE

After trying the handle, Vicker quickly found the door to be locked. Since the man inside that room was still screaming his head off and dodging whatever was being thrown at him, the marshal decided against trying to talk to him. Before he could ask, he saw Clint step up to the door and lower his shoulder.

While Vicker held his gun at the ready, Ben pressed himself flat against the wall with his eyes clenched shut.

Clint rammed into the door with his shoulder, cracking it open on the first try. The moment he charged into the room, Vicker came in right behind him.

"What the hell's going on in here?" Vicker growled.

Just as the last word was coming out of his mouth, he saw a man dressed in dirty britches wheel around to point a gun at him. Vicker took quick aim, but knew he would catch a bullet even if he did beat the other man and shoot first. They were just too close to each other for either of them to miss.

Earl's face was twisted in an angry mask. His hair was mussed and coarse stubble sprouted from his chin. In his left hand was an Army-model Colt that was bigger than the hand wrapped around it. Vicker took all of this in within the blink of an eye.

When he blinked again, Earl was being knocked off his feet.

Clint had charged at the half-dressed man from the side. Like a child's ball rattling inside a box, he'd rolled through the door, bounced off the wall, and then rolled straight into Earl. The moment he'd felt his shoulder impact against the half-dressed man, Clint had wrapped his arms around Earl's midsection and kept his feet pounding against the floor.

Although Earl spit out a bunch of grunted obscenities, he couldn't prevent himself from being knocked off his feet. His finger clenched reflexively around his trigger, but the big pistol's bullet punched a hole in the wall well away from where anyone was standing.

Clint felt as if he'd pushed that man half a mile before Earl's side slammed against a chest of drawers. All that time, he was expecting Earl to wriggle free or point that gun straight down into his head. Clint did hear another shot or two, but didn't feel the bite of any bullets. Before he could celebrate too much, however, he saw Earl's Colt swing upward just as he'd feared.

A few options flashed through Clint's mind. The first was to draw his own modified Colt and put Earl down for good. But since he'd already declined that option in favor of charging Earl head-on, it didn't make much sense to take it now. His other option wasn't too appealing either, but it was all he had left.

Clint reached out with his left hand to grab hold of Earl's gun arm. His fingers wrapped around the man's wrist just in time for him to force Earl's hand toward the ceiling before he pulled his trigger again. The Colt bucked and spit its lead into the ceiling. From there, Clint pulled Earl's arm toward him while swinging his right fist.

Between the strength behind that punch and being

pulled into it, Earl was almost knocked out right then and there. But he was too riled up to be dropped that easily. He did, however, lose a tooth in the bargain.

Still gripping Earl's wrist, Clint shook out some of the sharp pains that were flooding through his right fist. His knuckles were bloodied, but he was more than able to pull the gun from Earl's grasp. Just as he was going to turn and toss the gun to Vicker, Clint felt another source of pain blast through his lower body.

Earl had gritted his teeth and snapped his right leg up to viciously knee Clint in the groin. His aim was a little off, but he still managed to deliver a powerful blow to Clint's lower abdomen. The moment he saw Clint start to crumble, Earl raised his free arm so he could drive his elbow down onto Clint's collarbone.

Earl stopped just short of making his strike when he felt the touch of an iron barrel against his temple.

"That'll be just about enough of that," Vicker snarled.

Earl stayed still. His fist was still clenched and his elbow was poised over Clint's neck. His eyes kept darting back and forth between the marshal, the man that still had ahold of him, and the woman huddled at the back of the room.

Clint didn't need to be told to get out of harm's way. He could feel the impending blow as surely as if he had eyes in the back of his head. It took a bit of wrangling, but he disentangled his arms from Earl's and then took a few steps back.

"Lillian?" Vicker said over his shoulder. "Are you hurt?"

The dark-haired woman was barely covered by a flimsy silk slip that had already slid off of one shoulder. Even with the smell of burnt gunpowder still hanging in the air, the sight of her generous body wrapped in such a way was more than enough to distract the men in that room.

When Clint caught sight of her, he couldn't help but let

his eyes roam from the curves of her large breasts, down along her solid thighs, and back up again.

"I'm not hurt," she replied in a voice that cracked under the strain of her recent screaming. "But that's only because that limp-dicked asshole is such a lousy shot!"

"You fucking bitch." Those words rumbled up from the back of Earl's throat and drifted out through clenched teeth. At that moment, his eyes didn't see Clint, Marshal Vicker, or anything else in that room that wasn't wrapped in silk. His eyes focused solely upon Lillian, and he wasn't going to let anything stop him from getting his hands around her throat.

Clint recognized that look in Earl's eyes half a second before Earl lunged. Unfortunately, Vicker was still looking in Lillian's direction and wasn't able to step aside before he was being knocked aside.

It took every bit of speed Clint had to catch up to Earl before he made it across the room. It was pure stubbornness that kept him from drawing the Colt. He'd gone this far to bring this man in alive and he wasn't about to give up now.

Vicker stumbled back a few steps before righting himself and sighting along the barrel of his .45. Before he could pull his trigger, Clint and Earl were tangled up once again like a couple of bobcats that were fighting over a strip of meat.

As he choked on one vulgarity after another, Earl reached out for Lillian again and again. Every once in a while, he felt something holding him back, which caused him to send a quick fist or elbow in that direction. Clint managed to dodge the first few of those fists and elbows, but that became impossible once he got close enough to get both hands on his target.

One of Earl's wild punches caught Clint in the neck, but it was more of a vicious swat than anything else. That was followed by an elbow, which robbed Clint of his next few breaths. Clint weathered this storm without answering back until he got into a prime position. Once he was there, he allowed himself to cut loose.

The first thing Clint did was push forward with both arms to knock Earl away from Lillian. Next, he took a swing at the man's chin, which knocked the mean look clean off his face. Although he was stunned, Earl still moved to get back into the fight. That stopped when Clint delivered a solid hook to his jaw.

The final punch to Earl's lower stomach was a little bit of revenge for the aching that still raged in the bottom of Clint's own gut.

When he looked up at her, Clint saw a beaming smile on Lillian's face.

"I don't believe we've had the pleasure," she said while extending her hand as though she was at a cotillion.

SIX

"The name's Clint Adams. I take it you're Lillian?"

"I sure am," she replied with a smile that would have been just as fitting if she was wearing a formal gown rather than a torn slip. "Are you two the help our marshal has been needing so badly?"

Clint turned to look over his shoulder. Sure enough, Ben had found his way into the room now that the dust was settling. Looking back to her, Clint said, "We're just lending a hand."

"Truth be told," Ben said as he hurried forward to stand next to Earl's unconscious body like a hunter posing next to a five-point buck, "we just can't resist tending to a damsel in distress."

Judging by the look on Lillian's face, those words had the same sickening effect on her as they had on Clint and Marshal Vicker. She did manage to keep from showing it as much as those other two, however. "Well, I appreciate the help," she said, making a point to look at Clint and Vicker. "Earl here obviously isn't such a gentleman."

Vicker walked over to where Earl was lying and took handcuffs from his belt. Clamping the unconscious man's wrists behind his back, the marshal asked, "What was the cause behind all of this? Earl's not usually the type to pitch a fit like this."

Now that Earl was obviously unable to do any more harm, Lillian let herself relax. She strolled across the room and disappointed all three men by pulling on a robe that covered her nearly from head to toe. "Earl's been sneaking in this place for months. Usually, he just has something to eat or buys a drink for one of the girls. Then, he started giving me the eye."

"Who could blame him?" Clint asked.

She smiled at him as she sat on a small padded chair next to her vanity. When she crossed her legs, she allowed the robe to come open just enough to display a pair of shapely calves and thighs. "He stuttered like a nervous schoolboy when I tried to talk to him. Then, about a week ago, he found some courage."

"The kind that comes from a bottle?" Vicker guessed.

"Maybe a bit," Lillian replied. "I think it was more of him walking around with a stiff dick for so long that he forgot how bashful he was." Those words seemed so out of place coming from Lillian's pretty mouth that it caused all three men to twitch.

Fishing a cigarette from a plated silver case, she put it between her lips and struck a match. "One night, I thought he was going to make some more small talk and he winds up asking me how much I charged for the full ride."

"And that surprised you?" Clint asked.

She shifted her eyes to look at him and only him. The glance turned into a stare, which turned into a sultry smile upon Lillian's face. "Men like him know what me and these other girls do for a living. Still, they get shy. The cowboys and gamblers that drift through town don't waste any time since they've been riding hard and will be leaving soon. Locals like Earl tend to fuss more about what others will think.

"Plus," she added while taking a pull from her cigarette,

"I don't accept every offer that comes my way. I charge enough to be choosy."

"And Earl was worried about not being chosen?" Vicker asked.

"That's right, Marshal. But Earl was sweet. I like it when men treat a lady like a lady."

"So what was the problem?"

That put a sour look onto her face. This time, when she put her cigarette to her lips, she drew in an angry, smoke-filled breath. "I charge for my time. A fellow can have ten minutes, half an hour, or an hour."

"Earl wanted the full ride," Clint pointed out.

"That's right," she said with a nod. "I recommended the ten minutes." Lowering her voice a bit, she explained, "Most men who sit and stare at me for that long can't hold out for an hour. Some can, but not Earl. A woman can tell these things. He got a little upset and came up with enough money to cover an hour, so I agreed. Why the hell wouldn't I?"

Glancing over to Earl's unconscious form, Vicker said, "Judging by his state of dress and yours, he should have been in a much better frame of mind."

"He sure should," Lillian said. "He showed me a pretty good time. I even showed him a few things, but he was going too fast. You know how that goes."

Smirking at the uncomfortable silence that came from the other three men, she continued. "He did his business in about fifteen minutes even after I warned him to slow down. He kept saying he'd keep going after a little rest, but he was through. I even sucked him real good for a bit, but that didn't get much more than half a rise out of him.

"When it was clear he wasn't good for anything anytime soon, I offered to let him only pay for the half hour. Stupid me, I actually felt bad for embarrassing him. I was real nice about it. After all, this isn't the first time this has happened. But he wouldn't have any of it. He kept trying to get on me and kept forcing me to kiss him here and there. He even started getting forceful."

"How forceful?" Vicker asked.

"Grabbing my hair and such. Shoving me around. Even then, I said he could pay for the ten minutes where he was actually hard and to get the hell out of my room." Shaking her head while breathing out a stream of smoke, she said, "He didn't like that."

"Is that when he shot at you?"

She squinted at the marshal for a second and shook her head. "He smacked me and threw me against a wall. I kicked him in the balls and called him a jackass with a limp noodle between his legs. That's when he shot at me. After that, I was doing my best to hide while throwing whatever I could at him. You boys showed up right around then."

"All right then," Vicker said as he rubbed his hands together. "I'll haul this one off to jail and let you know if you'll need to tell this story to the judge when he makes his way back in town."

She stood up and looked down at Earl as if she was about to spit on him. "He took his money back when he had his pistol out."

Vicker dug into Earl's pocket and pulled out a wad of folded bills. She took them and tucked the entire wad between her large breasts. After that, she smiled politely at each of the three in turn.

"Be sure to come back and pay me another visit," she said. "I give brave men like you a discount."

SEVEN

Lillian's door slammed shut, leaving Clint, Ben, Vicker, and Earl all standing out in the hall. Now that the noise had died down, a few tentative faces were peeking out from behind cracked doors. Vicker led Earl by the chain connecting his wrists, nodding assuringly to everyone he saw.

Standing at the bottom of the stairs, Claudia looked up at the group hopefully. "Is it all right to come out?" she asked.

"Everything's fine," Vicker told her. "Lillian's all right. You can all get back to . . . whatever you were doing."

Apparently, those were the words that the entire building had been waiting to hear. While they were still echoing down the stairway, doors flew open, voices started filling the air, and a piano started playing in another part of the house.

Earl was walking on his own two feet, but was staggering like a drunk that barely knew where he was. His face was swollen and bruised, but nobody looked at him with the slightest bit of pity. It seemed that everyone knew what had happened in that room.

"Looks like you won't have any shortage of witnesses," Clint said.

Vicker shook his head and shoved Earl toward the front door. "Doubt I'll need any. The judge don't come through these parts more'n once a month and he's already been through less than a week ago."

"So there won't be a trial?" Ben asked.

"I'll see what I can arrange. I might fine him or just set him up for a whipping. That ought to make Lillian happy."

Clint moved ahead to open the door before Vicker used Earl's face to do the job. When they stepped outside, the winds had died down a bit, but were still kicking up enough dirt to sting their eyes. "Where are we taking him?"

"I got a couple jail cells built onto the back of my office," Vicker replied. "If you two got other things to do, I can drag this one there without any help."

"We were going to get something to eat. Actually, this seemed like as good a place as any."

"Then enjoy yourselves. I appreciate the help. By the way, if either of you two are interested in making some money while you're here, I could use someone to keep an eye on this one while he sits in his cell."

That caused Ben's ears to perk up. "How much?"

"Since you helped out here, I could tack on a few dollars on top of the normal wage, but it ain't anything to retire on."

"I'll check in with you tomorrow."

Vicker was plainly disappointed with which of the two had accepted his offer, but he nodded all the same. "I'll be around."

With that, the marshal tipped his hat and shoved his prisoner down the street.

Grinning as if he was the hero of the day, Ben turned to face Clint and asked, "Did you hear that? Looks like we might stand to make some money here after all. I've got a nose for it."

"Yeah," Clint grunted. "You really sniffed out a mother lode in this place. Now, since you let me take all the bumps and bruises back there, why don't you pay for dinner?"

"I don't know. We only managed to cash in the bounties on half of the banditos we were after and some of that money already went to—" When he saw the look on Clint's face, Ben nipped his own sentence in the bud. "Tell you what. Dinner's on me!"

"It's a deal." With that, Clint turned on his heels and walked straight back into Miss Pryde's Varieties. Ben was following closely behind him.

"You hear what that fine piece of woman upstairs said?" Ben asked excitedly. "She said we'd get a discount."

"If you're worried about paying for our meals, I doubt you could afford her, no matter what the discount."

"Still," Ben said as he stepped into the whore house, "I think she'd be worth it."

Now that the party was back in full swing at Miss Pryde's, the place seemed completely different than the one they'd entered the first time. It was even louder than when they'd left it a few seconds ago. The biggest difference was that Lillian was now coming down the stairs as if she'd been expecting Clint and Ben to return all along.

Lillian wore a dark red dress that clung to every one of her curves, with beads that wiggled back and forth with every move she made. Her face was touched up to look good as new and her red painted lips curled into a welcoming smile as she locked eyes with Clint.

"I'm sure you're right about that," Clint breathed.

EIGHT

Half an hour later, Marshal Vicker was once again walking down the street that cut Taloosa in half. Tucking Earl into his cell was a simple matter of opening a door, throwing him in, and locking that same door. Earl only came around long enough to find his cot and pull himself onto it before passing out again.

Although he didn't like the thought of leaving a prisoner unattended, Vicker didn't have much choice. Besides, he planned on getting back to his office before Earl was able to think straight. Even so, he quickened his steps toward the little cluster of homes just outside of town.

There were four houses arranged together and Vicker was after the second one. It was a small place, but one of the newer ones. Holding his fist in front of the door, he paused and took a deep breath before knocking. Vicker felt more hesitation now than when he'd been about to charge into a room where shots had already been fired through the door at him. Even after letting out his breath, he didn't feel much better.

His knuckles cracked against the door in a quick series of knocks that he hoped wouldn't be heard. Figuring he'd stand there for the count of ten before walking away, Vicker closed his eyes and placed his hands upon his hips.

At the count of four, he heard a few quick steps inside the house before the door was pulled open.

Vicker looked up and put on the most comforting expression his face could manage. "It's Earl, ma'am. He's in a bit of trouble."

Clint pushed away a plate with the remains of his baked potato, a few scraps of vegetables, and a large T-bone that was picked clean of anything resembling meat. The first steak had already been cleaned away with his other plate. "Good Lord, that was a fine meal," he breathed.

Sitting across the table from him, Ben was so stuffed that he appeared to be drunk. He wobbled in his seat and kept both hands pressed against his belly.

Lillian sat between the two men and said, "Claudia knows every way there is to get to a man's heart. Putting them all under one roof has made her one of the richest women in the county."

"Try *the* richest woman," Claudia said as she stepped up to the table. After a bit of a laugh, she reached out to place one hand each on both Clint's and Ben's shoulders.

Clint nodded and patted Claudia's hand. "With cooking like this, it's no surprise."

"I worked in a place in Kansas for eight years," the madam said. "Damn near every man who left either went to gamble or get something to eat. I couldn't believe my boss wasn't providing those things under her own roof."

"Don't let her take all the credit," Lillian added. "You two haven't tasted my cooking yet."

Ben's eyes grew wide as saucers. Claudia nodded subtly in his direction before she said her farewells and moved on. Clint noticed that Lillian shifted her chair a little closer to Ben's side within the next few seconds.

"How long have you two been in Taloosa anyway?" she asked.

"Not long enough to remember the name of the place until you mentioned it," Clint said.

"I bet you won't forget it after you leave."

Leaning in to fill his nose with more of Lillian's scent, Ben said, "You bet your ass we won't."

Even though she'd moved close enough to practically sit in Ben's lap, Lillian kept looking over to Clint. Finally, her face lit up and she snapped her fingers. "Labyrinth, Texas!" she shouted.

Clint's head snapped back a bit at the sudden outburst. "Excuse me?"

"I knew I recognized you from somewhere," she said excitedly. "It's from Labyrinth, Texas. You've been there, haven't you?"

"Sure. Plenty of times. You know a man named Rick Hartman?"

The smile on Lillian's face grew even wider as she nodded. "Rick's a sweetheart! How's he doing?"

Clint leaned forward to put his elbows on the table. Before he could settle too much further into the conversation, it was cut short by Ben's curt tone.

"Sorry to interrupt," Ben said, wearing a look that made it clear that he couldn't be less sorry to interrupt. "But I was hoping to buy me and the lady some dessert. Since Clint is surely stuffed and wants to stretch out on a bed somewhere, maybe we could pick this up a little later."

Lillian glanced over at Ben and draped one arm around his shoulder. Patting his cheek, she said, "This one's just getting ready to ask me about that discount I offered. I do love the shy ones."

"I would like to get a room for the night," Clint said as he stood up from the table. "Any hotels you can recommend, or does Claudia rent rooms in this fine establishment as well?"

"No rooms for rent," Lillian replied. "She's saving that for when she expands this place a bit more. Try the Desert Sun over on Ridgeway."

"Much obliged. Ben, don't even think about asking me for money."

Now that he had the most voluptuous woman he'd ever seen in his lap, Ben wore a proud smile and stuck out his chest. "Don't be silly. I won't need to do anything like that." Suddenly, reality tapped him on the shoulder and he lowered his head to sneak a glance toward Lillian. "Will I?"

"You'll be fine, handsome," she said.

Clint left the dining room and found his eyes immediately drawn to a poker game being held in the next room. Just as he was thinking he should secure a room before anything else, one of those players got up and left his spot empty.

If enough folks came wandering into the desert on a night like this, Clint figured they needed a room more than him anyway. "Evening, gentlemen," he said as he stepped up to the table to fill that empty seat. "Deal me in."

NINE

For Clint, one hell of a long day turned into one hell of a long night. It was one of the few times he hadn't listened to his instincts, and he almost wound up paying dearly for it. Claudia was more of a genius than a madam and made a place that was awfully hard to leave. By the time he cashed in his chips and left the poker game, it was getting close to dawn.

He knew he should have gotten a room as soon as he was done with supper, but Clint had opted to try his luck at cards. Although he wound up ahead by a few dollars when the game was over, he was almost out of luck where the room was concerned.

Not only was the Desert Sun the only hotel in town, but it only had four rooms to rent. Three of those were already spoken for, and Clint just managed to step up to the front desk as another customer walked in behind him. If he'd lollygagged for a few seconds longer at that game, he would be sleeping in the cramped stall next to Eclipse.

As it was, he managed to get the last room for himself after a surprisingly prolonged bidding war with the customer behind him. The hotel owner was more than happy to sit back and watch the price go up. He was even happier to accept Clint's winnings to pay for the room.

If Clint wasn't so tired by then, he would have been angry as hell when he got a look at the room he'd bartered for. Lillian's closet was probably bigger than the last room at the Desert Sun, but it had a bed and that was all Clint needed.

He dropped onto the paper-thin mattress, thinking that a bit of sleep would make everything all right. A few minutes later, Clint was awakened by a frantic knocking on his door. He was too tired to remember much, but Clint saw Ben outside, begging for a place to sleep.

Even though he had something resembling a bed under him, Clint still wound up having to listen to Ben's snoring. Even that racket wasn't enough to keep Clint from dozing off a few moments after he lay down that second time.

When Clint peeled his eyes open again, he wondered if he'd gotten any sleep at all. The light coming in through the window was a little dimmer, but just about the same color. All he needed to do was sit up and his nose was almost pressed against the glass. Rubbing his eyes, Clint stared outside and realized the shadows in the street were coming from the opposite direction.

"Jesus," he grumbled while fishing the watch from his pocket. It took a few tries, but his tired fingers finally managed to flip open the watch's cover. When he saw that he'd been asleep for nearly ten hours, Clint grumbled a little louder.

"Jesus!"

Even though he didn't have any appointments for that day or evening, Clint still felt like he was going to be late for something. It just didn't sit right with him to sleep away that much of the day for no good reason. As he pulled on a fresh set of clothes, he reminded himself of everything that had happened since the last time he'd been able to sleep. That eased his nerves a bit, but not all the way.

What did make him feel a whole lot better was the fact that Ben wasn't in the room with him any longer. Of course, when Clint thought of all the possibilities that left, his stomach started to clench yet again.

He'd met up with Ben Cable less than a month ago, and Clint still hadn't decided what the man did for a living. At first, Clint thought Ben was a banker or newspaperman, simply due to Ben's slight build. After Ben's mouth had gotten himself and Clint into one hell of a fight with some drunk gunhands, Clint wondered if Ben was a struggling gunfighter.

Somehow, Ben had talked Clint into running down a group of banditos. This caused Ben to claim he was a bounty hunter, but by this time, Clint had known the man well enough to take everything he said with a grain of salt.

Although Ben didn't look for trouble, he was always looking for money. And looking for money was always a good way for a man to get himself into trouble. That sort of double-talk was Benjamin Cable in a nutshell. Despite his better judgment, Clint decided to try and find where Ben had gone before it was too late to clean up whatever mess the man had created.

He started at the front desk of the hotel. Tipping his hat to the old woman sitting behind the open register, Clint said, "Good morning, ma'am."

"Afternoon is more like it," she replied brusquely.

"It sure is. I don't suppose you've seen a fellow leave here, a few inches shorter than me, skinny with dark hair?"

"Sure. He left right when I got here."

"And when was that?"

"Eight this morning. He seemed like the respectable sort who didn't sleep the day away."

Clint took the barbed words with a polite smile and a shrug. "Happen to know where he went?"

"No."

"All right then. Thanks for all your help."

Since the old lady seemed to have gone on to better things before he was even done speaking to her, Clint didn't bother saying a farewell and simply left the hotel. His next stop was Miss Pryde's Varieties. Along the way, he got his first real look at the town of Taloosa now that the sun was out and the dust was mostly on the ground where it belonged.

It was the kind of town where a man could see the end of it no matter which way he faced. There were a few houses scattered here and there on the outskirts, but most of it was a collection of storefronts arranged on four streets. If all else failed, he knew he could search Taloosa from top to bottom without much effort.

It felt good for him to pull in a breath without getting a lungful of sand. Clint had come to the desert as a way to clear his head and stretch his legs for a spell. The open trail had many different kinds of freedoms, and riding through the desert could be a rare treat. So long as a man kept his bearings and knew how to survive, the open plains of sand and dry heat could be downright comforting.

The desert was a place where Clint could feel like he was the only soul on earth. Everyone needed to feel that from time to time. Even as he walked down the dusty streets of Taloosa, Clint still felt that lonely freedom as the sky shifted from orange to a dark, bloody red.

When Clint stepped into Miss Pryde's, he was greeted like a family member. Lillian even blew him a kiss while she led an eager customer up the stairs. She was gone before Clint could get a word out.

"Something I can help you with?" Claudia asked as she stepped up beside him.

"Actually, yes. I'm looking for my friend."

"That little fellow who kept Lillian up all night?"

"That's the one."

Pausing to look Clint up and down, Claudia asked, "You look like you just rolled out of bed."

"That's because I just did."

She nodded approvingly. "I knew you were my kind of man. That little one seemed pretty jumpy, though. He came by for a late breakfast and mentioned something about paying Marshal Vicker a visit."

Clint shook his head. "I should have known. Guess I started walking before my brain had a chance to wake up."

"Let me fix you up with an eye-opener," Claudia said with a wink. "I insist."

TEN

When Clint walked into Marshal Vicker's office, he found
it to be empty. The little room was almost twice the size of
his hotel room, which wasn't saying much. It was a
cramped space filled mostly by a desk, an empty coat rack,
and a locked cabinet that probably contained a few guns
and some ammunition.

"Hello?" Clint called into the room, even though he
could plainly see it was empty. "You here, Marshal?"

There was no reply, which meant nobody was hiding
under anything.

Clint was leaning through the doorway with one hand
on the handle and his other hand wrapped around a large
mug. He stayed there for another second before stepping
back out. The moment the door slammed shut, a voice
drifted from inside.

"Hello?" came the faint sound.

Shoving open the door, Clint looked inside. The office
was just as empty as it had been a few seconds ago.

"Hello? Who's there?"

Now that he had his head inside the office, Clint could
tell the voice was coming from another room. Since there
were no other doorways in the little office, Clint shut the

door again and walked around the small building. As soon as he got to the backside of the structure, he spotted the part of it that had been tacked on like a wooden afterthought.

Since the addition seemed more solid than the building to which it was attached, Clint figured it must be Taloosa's jail. He tested the narrow door, found it to be unlocked, and pulled it open.

"Oh, Clint, it's you!" Ben said as he stood with his back to a wall and his gun in hand. "You gave me a little fright there."

The jail reminded Clint of a smaller version of the little stalls where Eclipse and Ben's horse had been put up. Two cells were sectioned off by thick iron bars set into the ceiling and floor and a hallway went down the length of them. That walkway wasn't even wide enough for Clint to move along it without bumping against either the wall or some of those bars.

"Shouldn't you keep this door locked?" Clint asked.

"Lock's broken. The ones on the cell doors are strong as can be, though. What's that in your hand?"

Clint looked down at the mug he was carrying and lifted it. "Coffee. Claudia poured me some when I went in to check on her. It wasn't exactly what I expected when she mentioned an eye-opener, but it's doing a hell of a job."

"It smells great. She send along any for me?"

"No. What are you doing here?"

"I took Marshal Vicker up on that job offer. Don't you remember?"

"I do, but I didn't think you were the sort to watch Earl sleep instead of heading out of here. What about those banditos?"

After holstering his gun, Ben sat back down upon a little stool in the corner. The cramped space made him look twice his size since his shoulders, elbows, and knees all knocked against something or other before he got situated. "What about them?"

"You were the one who was so fired up to bring them in."

"Yeah, but you were just along to make sure I didn't get myself killed along the way."

"That's not true," Clint replied. "Well, maybe not entirely."

Once he rested his head against the wall, Ben looked like a plant wilting in the corner. His eyes were pointed in the direction of the cell that was directly in front of him. Inside, Earl was stretched out on the floor with his back propped against bars. His bloodshot eyes were straining in the shadows to see who had come in.

"Well," Ben grunted. "Since I was the one who got us lost, I thought maybe I should be the one to go to work to make up for some of our expenses. Besides, I'm almost flat broke."

"Actually, I think you managed to find a pretty nice little town. Now that we've got our bearings, we're not even lost anymore."

Earl's voice gurgled up like a spit bubble swelling up in a frog's mouth. "I wish you'd get lost right now, you son of a bitch."

"Hey!" Ben shouted as he kicked the bars with his heel.

The impact of Ben's boot was enough to rattle Earl's head and send him crawling to the other side of the cell.

"You can't do that," Earl grunted. "You ain't no deputy."

"The marshal said I could shoot you if you looked at me funny," Ben replied. "You think he'll mind about anything else?"

Still rubbing his head, Earl didn't have anything else to say. At least, not to Ben. "You tore up my face when I wasn't looking," he croaked to Clint. "You're a cowardly bastard and I'll settle up with you soon as I'm outta this damn cage."

Clint rolled his eyes and took a sip of coffee. "Does Vicker need any more help?"

"Nah," Ben said. "I'm doing pretty well."

"If you need anything, just let me know."

"So are you gonna stay around here? I mean, if you want to leave town, don't worry about me."

"I'll probably be going in the next day or two."

"Y'see?" Earl grunted. "Runnin' away like a real cowar—"

This time, Clint and Ben both kicked the bars, which almost put another bruise on the section of Earl's face that was pressed against them. As Earl reeled back and cursed into the palms of his hands, Clint tossed a wave to Ben.

"If a room opens up at the hotel, I'll reserve it for you."

Ben nodded. "Much obliged. By the way . . . thanks for sticking by me."

"Those banditos didn't shoot at us that much, Ben. Don't get all sentimental."

"No, I meant in that storm. If you would have gone off the way you wanted . . ." Cringing, he reluctantly added, "The right way . . . you'd be in Las Vegas right now and I'd probably be dead and buried in a sand dune. It was me that led us into that storm, but you led us out. I owe you for that."

"I know you do and I plan on seeing to it that you make good on it," Clint said. "Drinks are on you until further notice."

"You got yourself a deal."

ELEVEN

Marshal Vicker came and went throughout the night to check in on Ben. For the most part, all he saw when he poked his nose into the jail was Ben sitting in his regular spot and Earl fussing about in his cell. When he pushed open the door for the last time that evening, Vicker didn't have any surprises waiting for him.

"It's getting close to nine o'clock," Vicker said as he looked in at Ben sitting upon his stool. "Time for me to patrol the corner."

Even in his short time working with the marshal, Ben knew the corner in question was a spot where Vicker could see both the Armadillo Saloon and Miss Pryde's Varieties in the same line of sight.

"How much longer should I stay here?" Ben asked.

"At least until midnight. Longer if you'll be all right."

"I'll be fine."

After a few seconds of studying Ben, Vicker nodded. "Okay then. I'll check back in a few hours. You need anything?"

"How about some of Claudia's coffee?"

"I'll have some sent over. And don't get any ideas about accepting anything more than coffee."

Ben gave the marshal a crisp salute and sat up straight. After Vicker left, Ben heard a snicker coming from the cell.

"What's so damn funny, Earl?"

"You got yer nose so far up that lawman's ass, it's no wonder yer breath smells like shit."

"Real tough talk coming from a man who beats on women."

"I'll beat you like a woman if'n you come in here."

Laughing under his breath, Ben reached under his stool for a folded newspaper. "Just shut up and sit down like a good dog."

The next half hour or so was filled with grunted insults from inside the cell, but Ben had already learned to tune out the sound of Earl's voice. He just kept reading his paper to the meager light of the jail's single lantern and let the minutes tick by.

When Ben heard the light knocking sound, he didn't even look over the top of his paper. "Stop it, Earl."

"I didn't do nothin'."

When the knocking came again, Ben lowered the paper and looked toward the door. Sure enough, the sound was coming from there. If the jail had been any bigger, he might not have even heard it. Ben got up, folded his paper, and tossed it under the stool. "Behave," he said to the solitary prisoner.

Earl responded with a crude gesture.

The door came open fairly easily, making Ben wonder for at least the tenth time why Vicker never bothered to fix that lock. Those thoughts were pushed right out of his head when he saw the striking redhead standing outside.

"Uhh, can I help you?" Ben stammered.

She was about the same height as Ben and had a slender build that still maintained her natural curves. She wore weathered jeans and a leather vest fitted loosely over her purple, button-down shirt. At the moment, those buttons

were opened down far enough to give Ben a glimpse of her
firm, perky breasts. Her voice was low and smooth as silk.
"I'm here to see Earl."

"Why?"

The redhead's eyes flickered for a moment like a candle
that had flared up in a breeze. "Because he's gonna be my
husband. Marshal Vicker came to my house last night to
tell me Earl was here. He said I could visit him if I
wanted."

"Oh, yeah. The marshal mentioned something about
that." Ben stepped back and held the door open. "Come on
in. You're not, uh, carrying anything, are you?"

Her pale face might have been pretty under normal cir-
cumstances. Shoulder-length red hair was tied back into two
tails, framing a stern expression. Holding her hands out, she
said, "Earl's in jail for beating on a whore. I didn't feel like
going through the trouble of bringing him anything."

Behind Ben, the bars of the cell started to rattle as Earl
pushed himself against them. "That you, Kira?"

"Yeah, Earl. It's me." Turning to Ben, she asked, "You
going to let me pass?"

Ben's eyes moved along the lines of Kira's body. Her
hips made a tight curve beneath her jeans and her slender
legs seemed to sprout up from a pair of knee-high boots. "I
just need to be certain you don't have anything with you.
Marshal's orders."

Kira held open her vest and did a quick turn. She could
feel Ben's eyes lingering on her breasts and then her backside. "Good enough for you?" she asked.

"I guess."

"Hey, you asshole!" Earl shouted. "That's my wife yer
gawking at!" When he saw the look on Kira's face, Earl
backed up as much as he could. "Well . . . wife-to-be," he
amended.

Kira eased past Ben and walked past the first cell. When
she got to the second one, she stood there with her arms

folded across her chest. Staring through the bars, she didn't say a word or move a muscle until Earl really started to squirm.

Ben did his best to keep his smile from being too obvious.

Slowly, Earl worked his way to the front of the cell. "Good to see you, darlin'," he said while extending his hand to her through the bars.

Kira moved her head and one shoulder back just enough to evade Earl's hand. "Good to see me? While you're locked up like the pig you are for getting out of line with some whore?"

"It sounds worse than it is. That whore goaded me into—"

"You're too stupid to even deny you were with her!"

"I . . . uh . . . I mean . . ."

Shaking her head, Kira uncrossed her arms. "Actually, I did bring you something, sweetheart," she said with a smile. And without that smile wavering in the slightest, she lifted the front of her shirt so she could get to the gun tucked under her belt.

TWELVE

It took a moment for Ben to realize what was going on. Unfortunately, by the time he'd fitted the pieces together, it was too late to do much about it. Kira stood in front of Earl's cell with her feet planted a shoulder width apart. The gun in her hand was a small .32, which was more than enough to put the fear of God into Earl's soul.

While only turning her head slightly in Ben's direction, she said, "Make a move for your gun and I'll start shooting."

"P-put down your gun and there won't be a problem," was Ben's shaky reply.

"Just reach out and take hold of those bars in front of you," she said in an unwavering voice. "I want my husband-to-be to sweat for a little while."

"I can't let you—"

Kira pivoted and pointed the gun at Ben in the blink of an eye. "Do what I asked."

Reflexively, Ben wrapped both hands around the bars of the empty cell. He struggled to come up with something to say, which occupied him just long enough for Kira to reach out and pluck the gun from his holster. The move was one of the fastest he'd seen.

Without lowering her own gun, Kira turned and set Ben's pistol on the floor in the corner. She then kicked it under the stool where it could join the folded newspaper. "Sometimes I wonder why I agreed to marry you," she said to Earl. "My family asks me that question at least three times a day."

"We have plenty of good t—"

"Shut your mouth," she barked. Settling back into her calmer tone, she continued. "Maybe it was those few nights when you weren't drunk and you were actually a kind, gentle man. Maybe I thought I could grow to love you. Maybe I just wanted to marry someone so I wouldn't be alone. Even with all those doubts, I agreed to marry you and even started to look forward to it.

"But you could never stop drinking. You could never stop shooting off that big mouth of yours and you could never stop going into that goddamn whorehouse!" The more she talked, the angrier she got. Although her eyes were twitching and her breaths were becoming longer and deeper, her gun hand remained perfectly still.

"Not only that," she said, "but you couldn't even fuck those whores like a normal man! You had to smack them around like they were some kind of animals!"

Even though his hands were trembling, Earl still managed to get himself to speak. Of course, that wasn't necessarily a good thing. "There was just one whore, darlin'. She was the only one I went to them times, I swear."

Kira's eyes narrowed and her thumb slowly found its way to the hammer of her gun. "And you didn't even have the sense God gave a mule. Either that, or you just didn't care enough to bother covering your tracks or hiding what you've done. Even half a man would know to lie about something like this, Earl. Especially to someone you were about to marry."

"Someone I am about to marry," Earl corrected with a hopeful smile.

"No, Earl. Were." With that, Kira lowered her arms and pulled her trigger.

The gun barked once, echoing within the cramped jail until it sounded more like a clap of thunder. A bit of smoke puffed from the short barrel and the brief shower of sparks illuminated the surprised look on Earl's face.

When he saw that, Ben felt like he was watching Earl's picture get taken. Earl's face was lit up for a second, searing his shocked and pained expression into Ben's mind. When Ben's eyes shifted back to Kira, he found the redhead wearing the same stern expression. As he watched, that expression shifted into a hint of a grim smile.

"Try fucking your whore now, asshole," she said. "Looks like no woman will have to put up with that pecker ever again."

When Ben took another look at Earl, he was the one to put on the shocked expression. Ben had seen men shot before and he was expecting to see Earl's shirt soaked with blood, or maybe even another hole in Earl's head. Instead, what he saw was a dark red stain spreading across the front of Earl's pants.

Earl staggered back until his back hit the wall. One arm stretched out to press against the wall while the other reached down for the fresh wound between his legs. As his fingers curled a bit into the bloody mess, his shocked expression grew.

"M . . . my pec . . . pecker," Earl stammered. "You sh . . . shot m . . ."

"Here," she said while reaching into the front of her shirt. Kira gripped a small necklace and pulled it so the chain snapped from around her neck. She then tossed the necklace into the cell so it could slap against Earl's chest. "Shove that up your ass right along with your marriage proposal."

Earl's face was turning pale as newly fallen snow. Streams of sweat poured down his cheeks and dripped off the end of his chin. Both hands were clutched to his groin as he slowly eased himself down to the floor.

Holding the gun at hip level, Kira turned to Ben. "Step away from that door," she said. Her face had more feeling in it now and her eyes were practically begging Ben to follow the order she'd given.

"Easy now," Ben said as he held both hands out in front of him.

"Too late for easy. Just move."

That cold, steely look was coming back into Kira's eyes and the memories were still awfully fresh of what happened the last time it had been there. Trying not to listen to Earl's whimpering, Ben pressed his back to the wall and slid away from the door.

Kira kept the gun pointed at him. For every step Ben took away from the door, she took one toward it. They continued that dance until she was able to open the door and duck outside.

Only after the door slammed shut again was Ben able to pull in another breath.

THIRTEEN

Kira headed outside, doing her best to keep her gun in hand while also keeping it out of sight. The only place for her to tie her horse had been across the street, but that seemed like a mile away. It seemed even farther once she heard Marshal Vicker's voice boom through the air.

"Who fired that shot?"

Folks around town said they only needed one lawman since Vicker had ears like a bat and eyes like a hawk. Apparently, they weren't far from the mark.

The marshal ran toward the office as the jail's door was pushed open. Kira looked away from Vicker to see that Ben was standing in the doorway she'd just left behind. He'd also retrieved his gun from where she'd tossed it.

"Stay where you are!" Ben shouted.

Vicker drew his own .45, but didn't seem sure of where to point it. "What the hell's going on?"

"Earl's been shot!" Ben shouted. "She did it!"

"What? Who did it?"

"She did. The redhead right there!"

"Where did those shots come from?"

"Who's been killed?"

As more and more people started lending their voices to

the exchange, all of them blended into a big mess in Kira's ears. Before too long, she couldn't even tell who was saying what. All she could hear was the beating of her own heart and the pounding of her feet as she kept trying to get to her horse.

"Stop her!" That voice definitely belonged to Ben.

Now that they could see there were guns drawn, the other people who'd been shouting quickly shut up and stepped back.

Vicker turned toward Kira, but still didn't raise his gun. "Are you sure about that, Ben?" he asked.

"I saw her pull the trigger. She shot him."

"All right then," Vicker said as he brought up his .45. "I'll need you to stay where you are so we can sort this out."

Just as he got his words out, Vicker saw the gun in Kira's hand. By then, it was too late for him to move before she took quick aim at him and fired.

The shot cracked through the air and punched a hole in the dirt a few paces behind the marshal. With the dust still swirling at Vicker's feet, Kira used her free hand to quickly pull back the hammer so she could fire her pistol once more. Her second shot whipped through the air close enough to Vicker to make him duck and jump for some cover.

"What in the hell are you doing, Kira?" Vicker shouted as he pressed his back to a thick post supporting an awning.

But Kira didn't respond. Her eyes were tracking every bit of movement she could find and her pistol was wavering slightly between Vicker and Ben.

From inside the jail, Earl's voice floated out in a lingering howl of pain. He sounded like a wounded animal, occasionally tossing in a recognizable word amid the rest of his noise.

Suddenly, another shot cracked through the air that

didn't come from Kira's gun. Taking another step forward, Ben held his smoking pistol in an outstretched hand and sighted along the barrel.

"I think I got her!" Ben shouted.

Although the bullet had come close enough to crack the cold resolve on Kira's face, it hadn't been close enough to draw any blood. She took one staggering backward step, regained her balance, and swung her weapon about to take proper aim.

Ben saw that barrel coming toward him and sucked in a quick breath. Dropping to one knee, he pulled his trigger again and hoped for the best.

This time, Kira didn't even hear the bullet hiss past her. She was close enough to her horse that she could reach out and pull the reins free from where they'd been looped around a post. Once she got one foot into the stirrups, she could practically feel the wind blowing in her face as she made her escape.

But she wasn't riding off just yet.

Another shot thundered through the air, this one coming from the marshal. "Don't get on that horse, goddammit!" Vicker growled. "We can sort through this."

That last shot had put enough of a fright into Kira's horse that it rocked on its hind and forelegs while shaking its head. It wasn't enough to toss Kira to the ground, but it made it difficult for her to climb into the saddle. In order to buy herself a bit more time, she fired at the first target she could find.

Ben was just starting to get up from where he'd been kneeling when Kira's shot blasted toward him. When he saw her gun go off, Ben knew he couldn't do a damn thing about it. He waited for what felt like an eternity to feel hot lead boring a hole through his body, but it never came. Instead, a fresh hole was punched into the side of the jail.

Since he was still drawing breath, Ben took his time and aimed properly. Just as Kira was settling into her saddle,

Ben pulled his trigger. He knew he was on target even before he saw the blood spray through the air. She didn't crumple over, but she definitely knew she'd been hit.

There was a sharp sting in Kira's left leg somewhere between her hip and knee. That was followed by a heat that began spreading up and down beneath her flesh. More painful than that, however, was the notion that she might not be getting away after all.

Vicker had abandoned his cover and was standing in the street once more. "Don't do this, Kira!" he shouted.

Her horse was already facing the open end of the street and was aching to run away from all the gunfire. She knew she had a choice to make and less than a second or two to make it. Kira could either listen to Vicker's words and give up, or she could listen to every instinct in her body as well as every slam of her racing heart, which screamed at her to run.

Letting out a fierce breath, Kira turned and saw Ben taking aim at her. She fired a shot in his direction, dug her heels into her horse's side, and bolted down the street.

"Goddamn!" Vicker shouted as he started running down the street while firing his .45 at the horse's backside. Every time he sent a bullet after Kira, he sent a curse along with it. Even after his pistol was empty, he had plenty more colorful words to launch into the air.

With the gunshots echoing down the street, the sound of hooves pounding against the earth slowly faded away. Dust swirled in the air along with the gritty smoke of burnt gunpowder to stick in the throats of all the locals who started cautiously moving into the street. No matter how curious they were, they weren't stupid enough to bother Vicker as he angrily reloaded his gun.

"How the hell did this happen?" Vicker snarled. "Sounds like Earl's been blown into pieces. Where the hell were you, Ben?"

After fitting in the last fresh round and snapping the

cylinder shut, Vicker sighted down his barrel. But Kira's
horse was well out of range, so he lowered the weapon and
wheeled around to Ben. "I'm getting my horse and bringing you one as well," Vicker said. "This happened on your
watch, so you can damn well . . ."

When Vicker got a look at Ben, he fell silent and
dropped his gun into its holster.

Ben was on both knees now, clutching his midsection
and hanging his head low. Blood dripped from his hand,
flowing from a widening stain at his belly. When he spoke,
his voice was a strained wheeze. "I think . . . I think I been
hit."

FOURTEEN

The inside of Miss Pryde's Varieties was too noisy for Clint to hear the gunshots. In fact, with the ruckus of a live show starting up combined with the hollering coming from his own and some of the other card games, he might have missed the outbreak of a war. He did hear it when someone came running in to spread the word about the gunshots that were fired outside the marshal's office.

At first, Clint and everyone else thought there'd been a jailbreak. But Clint had been there not too long ago and was pretty certain Earl didn't have that kind of sand. His thoughts immediately went to the jail's only guard, which was more than enough to send Clint running from Miss Pryde's.

He barely even remembered covering the distance between the table where he'd been playing poker and the jailhouse. The only thing running through Clint's mind was the need to run faster. When he finally got to the jailhouse, he came upon the very sight he'd been hoping to avoid.

People were gathered around the solid addition to the back of the marshal's office. The narrow door was open and even more folks were clustered around it. The smell of gunfire lingered in the air, causing Clint's hand to twitch toward the modified Colt at his hip. When he saw who was stretched out on the ground, Clint wasn't sure if he wanted to take one step closer.

"Clint?" Ben asked in a weary voice. "That you?"

Now that Ben had moved, Clint walked over to where he was lying and knelt down beside him. There was an older man with his sleeves rolled up who appeared to be tending to Ben, so Clint made sure to stay out of his way.

"Yeah, Ben," Clint said. "It's me. What happened to you?"

"I . . . figured out a way . . . to screw up the easiest job I've . . . ever had." Although Ben smirked and tried to laugh, the effort caused him to wince in pain.

The older man with the rolled-up shirtsleeves placed one hand flat upon Ben's chest. "Don't move, son. Just lay back and take it easy."

Clint looked around for a familiar face and quickly found Vicker's. The marshal was leaning against the jailhouse with his thumbs hooked over his gun belt.

"Marshal, what happened to Ben?" Clint asked.

"He's gut-shot."

"Good Lord."

"It's not as bad as all that," the older man said.

When he saw the way Clint was eyeing the older man, Vicker explained, "That's Doc Cosgrove. I had him brought here as quickly as I could."

Cosgrove had a mess of short, white hair sprouting out from his head at several odd angles. The thick mustache that covered his upper lip was a smaller version of that same mess. "The bullet entered in the middle abdomen, but came out the other side. It's bad, but shouldn't be fatal."

Clint leaned forward so he could get a look at the wound for himself. Although he'd seen plenty of men shot, he wasn't an expert on the medical aspects. It looked bad to him, but he was more than willing to take the doctor's optimistic appraisal.

"How you feeling, Ben?" Clint asked. "You going to be able to hang in there for us?"

Ben nodded weakly.

"Good. Just let the doctor do his job."

"I'd be able to accomplish that much better if I wasn't forced to work in the street," Cosgrove said.

"You need us to help carry him somewhere?"

"That would be marvelous. Just try not to shift him too badly."

Between Clint, Vicker, Cosgrove, and a few others pulled from the crowd, Ben was loaded onto a makeshift stretcher and carried away from the jail. Fortunately, Cosgrove's practice was only one street over. Ben was delivered onto a clean bed in a matter of minutes. Once that was done, Cosgrove was shooing everyone but his assistants out of his office.

Now that the smoke had cleared and the wounded man was taken out of plain sight, the crowd quickly found more amusing ways to pass their time. Vicker made sure the few stragglers moved along, and wasn't too nice about it.

"Where are you going?" Clint asked once Vicker started walking down the street.

"I ain't a doctor, so I can't do much good in there. Besides, we got ourselves another body to carry."

Clint's heart skipped a beat. "What? Whose?"

"Come with me. I'll explain what I know along the way."

Clint followed the marshal back to the jailhouse at a fairly quick pace. As they walked, Vicker told Clint what he'd seen take place from the last time he'd left Ben, right up to Kira's blazing ride out of town. Vicker wasn't much for words, so the story was done by the time they'd completed the short walk back to the jail.

"So Kira is Earl's wife?" Clint asked.

"She was gonna be his wife soon. The nuptials were to be in just a few weeks, I believe."

"And she was the one who started all this shooting?"

"That's what Ben said when he came running out of the jail behind her, but I scarcely believed it."

"I guess it could have been anyone, seeing as how the front door to the jail doesn't even have a lock on it."

Vicker turned to Clint with a fierce expression on his face. "And it was your friend who let her bring a gun in to do the job."

"You might have warned him some crazy woman was on her way to pay Earl a visit."

"She seemed upset when I told her where Earl was and what he'd done, but I sure as hell didn't see this coming." Vicker let out an exasperated breath and shook his head. "Nobody could have seen this coming. Take a look for yourself."

Clint didn't need to ask for details. Stepping into the jail gave him more than enough for his senses to sort out.

FIFTEEN

Traces of gun smoke were still hanging in the air, but were overpowered by a much more powerful stench. Clint could instantly pick up the scent of blood mixed in with a pungent taint of urine. The smells weren't the only things filling the air, however. There was also the constant sound of Earl's whimpering voice as well as the scrape of his boots against the floor.

". . . someone help me," Earl groaned.

The cell door was already open and Vicker stepped inside. "I'll need some help here, Clint."

"Did he get—?"

"Shot in the pecker?" Vicker said to finish Clint's question. "Sure looks that way to me. You want to bring that stretcher in here?"

It took a few seconds, but Clint finally snapped out of the shock of laying eyes on poor Earl. Considering the last time they'd met, it took a whole lot for Clint to feel sorry for the man. Seeing Earl grabbing onto the bloody mess between his legs was enough to make any man feel sorry for him.

"How long's he been laying here?" Clint asked as he grabbed Earl's ankles.

Vicker gripped the prisoner under both arms so he and Clint could lift him onto the stretcher. "Hard to say."

"And why didn't you mention this while the doctor was here?"

"Because there's only one doctor here in town and I didn't want to divert his attention from helping a good man so he could tend to a piece of shit that got what he deserved." As he said that, Vicker all but dumped Earl onto the stretcher and took hold of the poles.

Clint lifted his end and they started walking out of the jail. "He could have bled to death, you know."

"That or a bullet in the skull might be a blessing to him right about now."

"I see your point, but still . . ."

"Earl's been stirring up shit since I've started patrolling these streets as a keeper of the peace. How he wound up with someone like Kira is beyond me. I guess some bastards get luckier than others."

"Sounds like you know this Kira pretty well."

After glancing behind him to make sure he wasn't about to back into a water trough, Vicker shrugged and kept moving the stretcher along the side of the street. "We never broke bread or anything, but she was a good woman."

"Good women don't put a bullet into someone as they ride out of town after shooting their future husband in the balls."

Just hearing Clint say that was enough to get Earl squirming and moaning with renewed strength.

"Yeah. I don't know what the hell she was thinking," Vicker said. "On the other hand, I'm surprised it took her so long to reach the end of her rope where Earl was concerned. I seen women stick by assholes like him plenty of times, but she never struck me as that sort.

"Before you ask, I gave her every chance to give herself up, but I didn't let her go. Part of me still thinks that she wanted to get away from here without causing any more trouble."

Clint let out a humorless laugh. "Yeah. She strikes me as a real sweetheart."

"She fired her first few shots at my feet and over my head. She was just trying to warn me away."

"Maybe she likes you," Clint replied. "But she doesn't seem too sweet on Earl, or Ben for that matter."

Hearing Ben's name caused Vicker's brow to furrow. When he looked down, he didn't even seem to notice Earl's pained face. "Whatever I thought of her, all that went straight out the window when she shot that man. I'm sorry as hell about your friend, Clint. You got to believe me on that account."

Clint didn't say much else as he helped carry Earl to Doc Cosgrove's practice. In fact, once he got there, he put Earl where one of the doctor's assistants pointed and left. It was too soon to hear anything about Ben and he was sick of smelling blood.

"You don't have any more bodies stashed somewhere, do you?" Clint asked once Vicker was done answering the questions that came his way.

"No. That pretty much covers it."

"Then I'm going to get a drink."

SIXTEEN

After what he'd seen at the jailhouse, there wasn't much more that could hold Clint's attention for the rest of the night. His thoughts kept drifting back to Ben and the grisly sight inside Earl's cell. Clint wanted to be somewhere he could be left alone, so he steered clear of Miss Pryde's. The Armadillo Saloon was close by, so he lowered himself into an empty chair and ordered a beer.

The brew was salty and deposited some sort of sediment at the bottom of his mug, but he drank it down all the same. Before too long, someone approached his table who wasn't the middle-aged woman who'd brought his drink.

"Thought I might find you here, Clint," Vicker said. "Mind if I sit down?"

Clint replied with a shrug, which was good enough for the marshal.

After signaling for some whiskey to be sent over, Vicker let out a tired breath and settled into his chair. "Unless things have vastly improved recently, that beer's about half a notch over dirty river water."

"They haven't improved."

"Then perhaps you'd like to join me for a whiskey?"

"No, thanks."

Vicker nodded and kept quiet until his drink was brought over. Only after taking a sip did he bother trying to strike up conversation again. "I know I ain't your favorite person right now, but you got to believe I didn't want Ben to get hurt. Hell, I figured he would just have to keep Earl from messing up his cage too much and that would be it."

Slowly, Clint started to nod. "I know. I've been thinking about all that while I've been sitting here. You could have let someone know a little sooner about Earl, though. No man deserves to sit and suffer like he did."

Picking up his glass, Vicker looked at the healthy portion of whiskey that remained before draining it all in one gulp. He set the glass down and let out a haggard breath. "You want to know something? I looked into that jail when Ben was being tended to and thought ol' Earl was dead."

It took a moment of studying the man's face for Clint to realize that Vicker was completely serious. "But, when you brought me back to the jail, you said—"

"I said we had another body to collect. I figured we'd be hauling him off to the undertaker's. I damn near jumped out of my boots when Earl let out that first howl. He must have been passed out when I looked in on him before."

Clint studied the marshal for a little bit before saying anything. Then, when he got a pretty good feel for the man, he let out a laugh that shook him from his shoulders right down to his boots. At first, Vicker wasn't amused. But the more he listened to Clint laughing, the harder it was to keep himself from joining in.

It was as much of a tension breaker as the drinks in their hands. Once the laughter finally passed, both of them felt a little more human.

"You struck me as a good lawman, Marshal."

"I'm a hell of a lawman. I guess I'm just not the man you want around if you just got your dick blown off."

Once more, they broke into laughter. Only this time, it was a little easier to cut it short.

"Lord help us for laughing at this shit," Vicker said.

"It's either that or stew about it. Either way, we did what we could when we had the chance," Clint replied. "Nobody can fault us for that."

"If it was anyone else but Earl, I wouldn't be so quick to—"

"No need to explain. Sometimes there's just nothing else to do but laugh at something when it's all said and done."

Vicker nodded and waved toward the bar for another whiskey. "Your friend is hanging in there, just so you know. The doc had him patched up and resting. He wants to keep an eye out for infection, but says Ben should be up and around before too long."

Raising his mug in a toast, Clint said, "Good news. What about Earl?"

Vicker winced reflexively at the very thought of what he was going to say. "I couldn't stick around for all of it, but his . . . umm . . . let's just say that Kira was a hell of a shot."

Clint winced at that one too.

"Besides blasting off his pecker, she took a chunk out of his leg. I don't know how Doc Cosgrove can patch that up, but it looks like he should be able to keep Earl from bleeding out."

"I've seen a lot of men get shot in a lot of places," Clint mused. "But that's the sort of thing that gunfighters don't even like thinking about."

"I been on battlefields before and the thought of that poor bastard still puts a chill down my back." After a moment of silence, Vicker took a drink from the fresh glass of whiskey that was brought over to him. "Anyway, that was only part of the reason I wanted to have a word with you. Mind if I ask you a personal question, Clint?"

"After what we've been talking about just now, I can't see how it could make me squirm any more."

"How well do you know your way around a gun?"

The wary smile that had been on Clint's face dwindled down to nothing when he heard that. "I can hold my own."

"Are you a wanted man?"

"No. What brought this on?"

"I noticed the gun you carry isn't just something you got from a case somewhere. It looks like the weapon of a man who knows how to use it."

"I'm impressed. Most folks wouldn't be able to tell the difference."

"That model Colt didn't come with that sort of casing on the grip," Vicker explained. "Since there ain't no fancy engraving on it, the only reason for you to bother switching it out rather than just replacing it with what should be there is if you made some other modifications."

Clint nodded. "I did."

"And that usually means that you care enough to tinker with your weapon to get the best performance out of it, which brings me around to you being a professional."

"I'm good with a gun, Marshal. Professional is stretching it. Now maybe you could answer *my* question. Why do you need to know any of this?"

"Because I don't want to hire a gunman and I don't want to send some killer out with my blessing." Vicker pulled in a breath and bowed his head. When he looked up again, his eyes were the color of ice. "I'm going to put a price on Kira's head and I want you to be the first man to get on her trail."

SEVENTEEN

"Are you sure about that?" Clint asked. "A while ago, it sounded to me like you might be sweet on this woman."

Vicker's eyes remained cold. His voice even took on its own chill. "I thought she was a good woman. Obviously, I was wrong about that. She shot a man in my jail and shot a man who works for me. There's no way I can let that pass. No way in hell."

"You don't have to let it pass," Clint said. "But putting a price on her head is another matter entirely. Do you plan on making this known to anyone but me?"

Vicker nodded.

"Then it's a bounty," Clint said. "And the men that will try to cash it in won't give a damn if she's a woman or if she used to be a good one. The fact that she's a woman might make it awfully rough on her if she's caught."

"She should have thought about that before getting so gun-happy in my town."

There was no doubt that Vicker was serious. There wasn't a trace of doubt on his face or in his eyes that Clint could see, and he was sure taking his time in looking for it. After a while, Clint couldn't decide whether or not he was starting to look a little too hard.

It was that last fact that Vicker picked up on when he said, "You're questioning me awfully hard for a man whose friend is laying shot up on a table not far from this spot."

"I'm just making sure you won't be changing your stance on this once it's too late to do anything about it."

"I won't be changing anything," Vicker said sternly.

"And I want to make certain you know what you're doing before you put a price on the head of a woman you seemed to care for at one time."

"At one time, Clint. Those are the key words. I was lenient on her once before, which is why there are two men who got shot instead of just the one.

"As far as the bounty is concerned, I've heard some of the stories of a few of the other women who have been caught by the sort of men who go after those rewards for a living. That's why I wanted to give you a head start. You strike me as the sort of man who could get the job done the way it needed to be done and quickly enough to beat the pack of wild dogs before they come after their prize."

"Why not just do the job yourself?" Clint asked.

"If I was able to leave this town by its lonesome, I might just do that. This may not be a very big place, but it does need law."

"Any chance you might be able to hold off on making the price on her head known so I can have a chance to go after her on my own?"

Vicker winced slightly and said, "I hesitated once and look what happened. If she got away or did any more damage because I hesitated again, I wouldn't be able to live with myself."

"That's understandable, but plenty of bounty hunters will be going after her. Not only because they'd like the thought of having a woman at their mercy, but because she'll seem like easy pickings."

"Like I already said, Clint. She used up any favors when she shot Ben."

Clint could see that Vicker wasn't going to budge. He'd said his piece and made plenty of sense. Although Clint could understand where the marshal was coming from, part of him just didn't like the thought of putting a woman, any woman, up for grabs for the sort of men that would come after her.

As if reading his thoughts, Vicker said, "I dealt with a few bounty hunters. No matter how soon I put up the notice, it'll take a while for the word to spread. She can't be that far away, so any typical man should have a decent chance at tracking her down. Besides, I know who you are and The Gunsmith isn't no typical man."

Clint leaned back and nodded slowly. "And here I thought you only knew my first name."

"I did a bit of checking."

"So why ask me if I was good with a gun?"

"You should know well enough that you can't always trust what you hear. I heard you were a deadly shot and a straightforward fellow. I just needed to test the waters."

"And?"

Now Vicker smirked a bit. "And sometimes you can believe the things you hear. So, are you going to be the first man on this trail?"

Clint's mind flashed to the sight of Ben lying in the street with blood soaking through his shirt. "Yeah. I'll do it."

EIGHTEEN

Clint was fortunate that Kira had bolted from a town as small as Taloosa. Almost half the folks in town had seen her ride away and there wasn't much of anything in their line of sight. Clint only had to talk to a few of those people to get a detailed account, which didn't vary much from one local to another.

Kira didn't have any corners to turn and no other places in town to ride. She'd thundered straight down one street until it opened into open road, turned past a cluster of three houses, and then headed west into the desert. As long as there wasn't another windstorm, Clint figured he could catch up with her in less than a day.

Since he was already well rested, he got his supplies and headed out while the sun was on its way down. He knew which way Kira had headed, had a good description of her, and had a pretty good idea of where she was going. All he could think of as he put Taloosa behind him was how much Ben would have liked to be in on this job.

Comparing the desert to how it had been when he and Ben had arrived was like comparing the same stretch of ocean when it was calm to when there was a typhoon going on. If he didn't know any better, Clint might have thought that he'd ridden into a completely different part of the country.

But while the winds might not have been kicking up a sheet of blinding sand, they were still blowing. That meant whatever tracks Kira might have left were getting filled in. As for any brush or trees, all Clint had to work with was a few stands here and there along with some stubborn sticks sprouting up from the dust.

Clint had tracked plenty of people before. But this time, he simply didn't have many tools at his disposal. It was going to be a tough job. Fortunately, it was going to be just as tough for any other hunters who decided to try and take a shot at Kira's bounty.

As the sun dipped below the horizon, the sky turned a deep shade of purple. The air became cooler as the sky shifted to the blood red of dusk, putting a second wind into Clint's sails. He pulled Eclipse's reins and brought the Darley Arabian to a stop.

"All right, boy," he said under his breath while patting the stallion's neck. "If I were a woman on the run, where would I go?"

His eyes moved back and forth over the horizon, taking in the sights and scrutinizing every last one. When tracking someone on the run, there were certain things to do to get ahead of them. Of course, that was assuming that the runner knew what they were doing. Although he'd heard plenty of things about Kira, not one of them made him think that she was an experienced fugitive.

She was probably scared and still trying to collect herself after shooting Earl. Pulling a trigger had a way of rattling a person. Even Clint still felt those effects, and he knew he had a lot more experience than her. Then again, if she was able to blast Earl in the groin and walk out of that jail, this woman had a bit more sand than normal.

Clint let out a breath. Already, the air was cooling enough for wisps of it to form in front of him. It was going to be a cold desert night and he couldn't afford to let it slip away without making progress. Suddenly, he realized that his eyes had settled upon a jagged shape in the distance.

Until now, that shape had blended in with the rest of the horizon. At the moment, with the sun's glare away from his eyes, Clint could see that he was looking at a small rock formation. It wasn't much, but it was just big enough to poke its head up from the ocean of sand that had drifted on top of it.

"What do you think, boy?" Clint asked out loud. "Does that look like a good place to spend the night?"

Eclipse didn't have any answers, but he did seem plenty eager to get moving again. The Darley Arabian shifted his hooves to keep on top of the sand, which made him even more anxious to head out.

Clint started laughing to himself as he reached down to take the spyglass from his saddlebag. "Sometimes, I think a bit too much for my own good," he muttered as he lifted the spyglass to his eye.

As Clint studied the desert in front of him, he looked for any trace of a fire or other movement. He'd been looking for a dust trail the entire time, but it was getting about that time when someone out there might start making a fire. There was plenty of scraps of wood to be collected, all of which were dry enough to make plenty of smoke when they were burned.

"No fires. At least, not yet. Guess those rocks are our best bet."

Eclipse felt the spyglass get dropped back into the saddlebag, and was already moving when Clint flicked the reins. After a few long strides, the stallion broke into a full run. His strong legs thundered through the sand without fail. Where other horses might have slipped or lost their footing, Eclipse only added to his forward momentum. He was born to run and that never shone through more than right now.

Clint was familiar with the tricks that could be played on a man's eyes. Those tricks were almost doubled once a man set foot in the desert. At first glance, he figured he could reach those rocks just after the last bit of sunlight had left the sky. Now, Clint thought he might have some sunlight to make searching those rocks even easier.

For a moment, Clint thought he was back in the middle of that windstorm. Eclipse's hooves were kicking up so much dust that it stung Clint's eyes and stuck to the back of his throat. But rather than hold Eclipse back, he simply held on and let him run. Before too long, Clint had to fight to keep himself from letting out a holler as he shot across the sand like a bullet.

That rock formation came toward him as if it was being reeled in on a fishing line. Clint held onto his hat and leaned down low over Eclipse's neck. He might not have had this job in mind, but moments like these were why he'd come to the desert in the first place.

In fact, Clint was feeling so good that he was already wondering how he might spend that bounty money once the job was over. Some thought that was a good way to jinx yourself. Clint's spirits were too high to be so superstitious.

NINETEEN

The sky over Clint's head looked like a blood-smeared shroud. It was black for the most part, but with a few red streaks as the sun was slowly being swallowed up. Eclipse was tethered a little ways back, allowing Clint to move on foot and allow his senses to stretch out in every direction.

While his blood was still pumping through his veins in a rush, he wasn't as hungry for speed as he'd been while in the saddle. On the contrary, one hand remained on the butt of his holstered Colt while his other hand remained stretched in front of him and lowered toward the ground. He crouched down low so he could spot any tracks that remained. So far, he wasn't having any luck.

Without much to get in the way of the passing breeze, Clint's ears weren't picking up on the rustle of any leaves or the waving of any branches. Apart from the sifting of one layer of sand against another, all he could hear was the lonely howl of a slowly stirring wind.

Clint made it all the way to the top of the rocks without seeing so much as a single thing to catch his eye. There were no tracks, no horse droppings, not even anything that might have fallen out of a pocket to mark that anyone at all had been there.

Perhaps he was being a little too optimistic to think he
would catch up to her so soon, but Clint couldn't help feeling disappointed. Even so, he hadn't come all this way to
simply climb over the top of those rocks. Desert rock for-
mations were oftentimes more than just a pile of stone. All
that sand and wind had a way of cutting into the sides of
rocks like those.

Clint was looking for a cave. After all, if he was on the
run, that's exactly the type of spot he would look for to
take a rest.

Keeping his feet sliding lightly against the sand to cover
the sound of his steps, Clint kept moving and worked his
way to the base of the rocks. As he'd figured, there was
plenty more to the formation than what he'd spotted from
afar. In fact, the formation dropped off on the back side
with a drop of just over seven feet.

Clint pressed his belly against the sand and made his
way to the edge of that drop-off like a snake slithering
through the grass. When he got there, he held onto the lip
with both hands and slid just far enough to get a look over
the side.

There was a cave, all right. It wasn't much of one, but it
was big enough to hold a person or two. It might have even
been large enough to hold a small horse. Kira rode a small
horse. Clint had learned that much when talking to the locals who'd seen her ride from town.

She could very well be in there, and there was only one
sure way for Clint to know for sure.

Clint held onto the upper lip of the cave while curling
his legs up underneath him. He slid down along the slope
of the drop-off while working his hands, one over the
other, in that same direction. He made it to the other side
without stirring up much in the way of noise. After taking a
moment to get himself crouched and on sure footing, Clint
took a look at the mouth of the cave.

A small horse might have been able to get in there, but

not without scraping the back of its neck up pretty good. He couldn't hear anything coming from inside the cave, but that didn't mean much. If the cave went in too far, Clint knew he was just giving her more time to dig in and prepare for him.

Kira had already shot two men. Woman or not, she was dangerous and she was riled up to boot. Although Clint didn't draw the modified Colt, he kept one hand close enough to it so he could clear leather with little more than a thought.

After digging his hand around in the sand at his feet, Clint found a pebble and pitched it into the cave. It clattered against the dry rock loudly enough to make a few echoes. Other than that, there wasn't anything else happening inside that cave.

Slowly, Clint worked his way to the opening. The sun had been gone long enough for his eyes to become somewhat adjusted to the darkness. Then again, darkness took on a whole new meaning in the desert. There wasn't much any man's eyes could see in those thick, unmoving shadows.

The time for feeling out the situation had come and gone. Clint let out a breath, kept his head low, and rushed into the cave. Just as he'd figured, it was cramped inside the little space, but it went back a little more than he'd expected.

Just as his feet had come to a stop, he heard something else scraping against the cave's floor. Clint couldn't see whoever was moving, but that didn't keep him from scuttling back until his back knocked against the closest wall. The uneven surface jabbed between his shoulders, causing his head to crack against a piece of jutting stone.

When he came to a stop, Clint's skull was aching and his Colt was in his hand. The scraping steps were rushing toward him, but before he pulled his trigger, he wanted to get a look at who was headed his way.

Clint stopped just short of taking a shot, but managed to hold off at the last moment. It was hard to see exactly what it was thanks to the shadows. It might have been a large rabbit, or even some kind of bobcat, but it most certainly wasn't Kira.

"Damn," Clint muttered as the animal bolted out of the cave and ran away.

Just to be certain, Clint worked his way further back into the shadows. He could see a bit more now than when he'd first come in, and could even make out most of the interior's uneven surfaces. The cave went back another five paces or so, with the ceiling angling steeply down every step of the way. There was no way a horse could spend more than a few seconds inside such a space. Besides that, Clint didn't find a lick of evidence that anyone had even tried.

Walking out of the cave, he looked around and saw nothing but the same sand he'd been looking at since his ride had started. There was a jackrabbit perched on a smaller rock not too far away. He couldn't be certain if that was the same critter that had bolted from the cave, but Clint didn't much care. He drew the Colt and killed it with one quick shot.

At least he would walk out of there with a good meal.

TWENTY

Kira felt as if she'd been riding for weeks on end. Although the gunshots were still ringing in her ears, the details of her escape from Taloosa were beginning to smear like a painting that had been left out in the rain.

She'd lived in Nevada all her life. To her, the desert was just another piece of land. Strangers and folks from out East said every foot of sand looked the same. That just wasn't the case. She knew those drifts, dunes, and rocks the way a Colorado native knew every turn of their local streams. She wasn't, however, so experienced at running from the law.

While she hadn't exactly acted on a whim, Kira had never expected her actions to draw so much heat. Looking back on it, that was a foolish thing to think, but she just didn't know any better. Even with all that in mind, she didn't regret a single thing.

That wasn't true, she realized as she gripped onto her reins a little tighter. She thought back to that new fellow she'd found inside the jail and regretted that he'd been there at all.

Most times when she came by to visit Earl in that place, the front door was open and Marshal Vicker watched from outside. The lawman had even left the cells unattended when the only thing they contained was a drunk or two.

Kira may have been assuming too much to think that things would have been so different, but there was no way for her to know that Vicker would have hired a deputy at this particular time. She shook her head at that bad turn of luck. Beneath her, Kira's horse was straining more and breathing heavier.

"Just a little ways more," she said to the animal.

In a strange way, she felt bad for lying to the horse. She knew it couldn't understand her, but there was no reason for it to take comfort from her voice. Once they got to where they were going, they would have to turn right around and ride some more. Kira could only pray that the horse wouldn't drop over from sheer exhaustion.

When she saw the familiar shapes drawing closer, Kira pulled back on the reins and slowed the horse down. In order to give the animal a bit more time to rest, she let it come to a stop before she dropped from the saddle and ran toward the nearby house. There wasn't anyplace to tie off the reins, but she knew the horse wouldn't leave her. Besides, it was too tired to get far anyhow.

There were a few other houses in the area, but hers was a little ways from all of them. She'd always liked being on the side that faced away from town. That way, she could always look out to the open spaces and let her mind wander. In more recent months, she'd spent that time dreaming of a time when she could just take off and ride away straight into those spaces.

She'd gotten her wish.

Now she just had to survive it.

A few of the neighboring windows had a flickering light behind them, but there wasn't much by way of movement. If she knew her neighbors, they'd probably just fallen asleep without turning down their lanterns. Just to be safe, however, Kira snuck up to the back door of her house and eased it open.

The subtle squeak of the hinges sounded like a child's screaming in her ears. Nobody else took much notice, so she tiptoed inside and shut the door. Once she was inside, she exploded into a furious set of motions that she'd been planning since she'd turned around in the desert and doubled back.

Her first stop was to grab a small bag. From there, she raced about her bedroom, gathering up clothes and her most precious belongings. That took a minute or two, after which she lowered her shoulder and practically rammed it against the post of her bed.

The bed scraped noisily against the floor and Kira dropped down to claw at one of the boards. It came loose after a few tries, allowing her to pull it up and snatch a small leather pouch secreted underneath. When Kira got that pouch in her hand, she stretched her arm out a little and closed her eyes.

After a few seconds of weighing the pouch, she smiled and nodded. Her fingers then tightened around it even more and she jumped to her feet. The pouch was stuffed beneath her belt and she left the bedroom. Without breaking stride, she grabbed the bag she'd packed and headed for the front door.

Rather than leave that way, she stopped short and pulled aside the curtain of the window next to the door. Her finger barely caused the material to move, but she shifted it just enough to get a look outside. Her breath steamed up the glass as she peered through it.

Things were just as quiet now as when she'd arrived. Although a few folks were moving here and there, none of them were coming anywhere near her house. Kira could see her own smile reflected in the glass as she eased the curtain back to cover the window.

It took every bit of restrain she had to keep from breaking into a run as she slipped out the other door. Once there were no more wooden planks beneath her feet, she gave in to her instincts and rushed to where her horse was waiting. She came up on the animal so fast that she almost spooked it.

Kira quickly calmed her horse with a few pats and climbed into the saddle. Once the horse had put some distance between Kira and those houses, she snapped the reins and urged the animal into a run. As much as she wanted to look back at Taloosa one more time, she fought back the urge to do so. Instead, she found a particular spot on the dark horizon and pointed her horse's nose toward it.

In the deep shadows she left behind, another figure on horseback kept pace with Kira. Although it could have overtaken her, the rider held back and was content to simply follow her into the desert.

TWENTY-ONE

The next day was a hot one by most everyone's standards. For those who lived in Nevada, however, it was just another day in the heat. Kira knew better than to try and travel too far in the brightest part of the day, and she left her shelter after only an hour or two of sleep so she could ride a bit further before stopping again.

When she felt her strength begin to bleed out of her as the sun beat down onto her face and back, she found another spot where she and her horse could get some shade. With her back propped against a flat rock and her hat pulled down low, she got some more rest while keeping one eye on the horizon.

Sweat poured down her face and she felt as if she was melting onto the rock the way a candle becomes melted onto its holder. She fed her horse some water from the palm of her hand while occasionally letting some trickle down her own throat. Bits of trail mix passed for a meal.

Although the day was hot and arduous, it helped her keep her mind focused on nothing but the present. The past was still a fresh wound for her, but at least it was being pushed to one side for the time being.

Once the sun began its descent, Kira got on her horse

and started moving a little faster. As the shadows began to form and the heat started to let up, she snapped the reins and tried to cover some real ground. All day long, she'd kept her eyes open for any sign that someone might be following her. The possibility of a posse crossed her mind, but she dismissed that with a grunting laugh.

Vicker didn't have enough men to form a posse.

Hell, Taloosa didn't have enough men of the kind that was needed to form a posse. As far as she could ever tell, it was a town of drunks, whoremongers, and those too lazy to find a better place to live. She would have moved on a long time ago if her situation hadn't been what it was.

Without meaning to, Kira fell into her own train of thought as she looked back to see where she'd gone wrong. It wasn't a very good time for reminiscence, however. She realized that for herself the hard way.

Since she'd been steering clear of the few trails wherever she could, Kira's horse was running on loose sand. Although the animal was used to the terrain, that also meant she couldn't hear any other riders coming up on her until they were nipping at her heels.

She caught a bit of movement from the corner of her eye. It was more of a shadow that seemed to peel off from behind a rock and rush toward her. In fact, the rider had been waiting there behind that rock for just this moment. When his moment came, he dug his heels into his horse's sides and reached out to grab her.

She let out a little yelp when she saw the stranger reaching out for her. Reflexively, she pulled hard on the reins to steer her horse away from the other rider. As she fought to get away from him, there was still a part of her brain that didn't believe the man was actually there.

She hadn't seen him coming until it was too late, even though she'd been waiting for an ambush since her escape from that jail. Fortunately, her horse was either quick enough or frightened enough to evade the other rider's grab. If not, Kira's reins might now be in the wrong hands.

Now that she could take a breath, Kira cleared her thoughts enough to go for her gun. The pistol was still tucked under her belt, but it snagged there when she tried to pull it free. Her heart slammed against her ribs as she pulled again and again at the weapon that was still wedged in its place.

"No, you don't," the rider said.

Kira was trying too hard to get her gun loose to focus on the man's face. In fact, she didn't even let out her breath until the pistol finally came free. Now that she was able to aim the gun, she turned to pick out her target.

When she twisted in the saddle and got a clear look at the other rider, Kira found herself looking straight down the barrel of the man's gun. He was still reaching out to grab either her or her reins, but his other hand kept his pistol tucked in close to his side.

The sounds of both horses' hooves beating into the sand was now mingling in Kira's ears, filling her head with a continuous drumming noise. Her gun was in hand, but she knew she wouldn't be able to fire a shot before the man beside her pulled his own trigger. The thought of that made every muscle in her body brace for the moment when she was shot.

Even though she was expecting it, the gunshot still made Kira jump in her skin. She let out a bit of a scream, but didn't feel the pain just yet. In fact, after a few seconds had gone by, she still didn't feel any pain. Judging by the look on the man's face riding beside her, he was the one in pain.

"Goddamn," the man grunted as he wobbled in his saddle.

Suddenly, Kira heard the drumming of hooves grow even more. She followed the other man's line of sight until she saw a second man come swooping in from her right.

This second man had his gun in hand and was aiming straight at her. Smoke and sparks issued from his barrel and something whipped through the air past Kira's face. She could hear a wet slapping sound and saw the first man twist so violently in his saddle that she thought for certain he was going to drop out of it.

Gritting his teeth and letting out a fierce curse, the first man gripped his reins with both hands and pulled his horse sharply away to the left. He fired a few shots over his shoulder, but those hissed far and wide from their intended targets.

The second man rode up a little closer and tipped his hat at Kira. He then used the barrel of his gun to point in the direction opposite from the one the first rider had chosen. She nodded and steered her horse that way. The rider who remained with her fell back just a little bit and kept his gun in hand. The pistol wasn't pointed at her, but it was plain to see that he could fire at any moment.

Kira found herself trying to think of a good time to take a shot. In the next moment, she couldn't believe what she was thinking. She also couldn't believe that she was following this stranger to wherever he was going. At the moment, however, it didn't seem like she had a choice.

TWENTY-TWO

After a few minutes of uneasy riding, the man sped up to come alongside Kira. Once again, he used his gun to point to a spot.

"Stop right over there," he shouted.

Pulling in a breath, she nodded.

Kira's mind raced once more. It felt as though it hadn't stopped racing for quite a while. She figured she could slow down and then try to run off, but there wasn't much of anywhere to run. Besides that, she had no way of knowing if the man's horse was better rested and could outlast her own. His horse had overtaken her and that other man fairly easily, which didn't bode well for her either.

Rather than try anything too stupid, she went to the spot and pulled back on her reins. Time would only tell how stupid a decision that was.

After her horse had come to a stop, the man circled around so his horse was standing directly in front of Kira's. He stayed in his saddle with his gun aiming at her across his own body.

"I saw the gun in your hand earlier," he said. "Hold it with two fingers and drop it to the ground."

When Kira started to hold out her gun, she saw the

man's hand tense a bit and his pistol come up as if he was adjusting her aim. That's when she realized she was holding her own gun in her hand instead of using the two fingers that he'd requested. Since she wasn't confident in her outshooting him in this situation, she adjusted her grip and dropped the gun to the ground.

"Are there any others?" he asked.

"No," she replied.

After a moment, he nodded. "Then climb down from your saddle."

Although she started to move, Kira stopped and asked, "What about you?"

"What about me?"

"If you're going to shoot me and steal my horse, I might as well just stay put."

"If I was going to shoot you, I would have done it a while ago."

She couldn't dispute that logic, but she still didn't like the idea of following his orders to the letter. "Are you coming down as well?"

"Yes." He looked at her carefully. Most of the man's face was covered by a dirty bandanna, much like most newcomers to the desert wore theirs. His eyes were intent, but not dangerous. Earl's looked more threatening when he came home from a night of drinking.

"All right," he said finally. "I'll come down at the same time. Fair enough for you?"

"I guess."

Slowly, both of them eased their way down from their saddles. The careful way they dismounted might have been funny if both of them weren't so worried about catching a bullet. Finally, their boots touched the sand. Kira stood with her hands held out to her sides while the man stood with his gun still pointing at her. His barrel hadn't wavered once the entire time he'd climbed down.

Kira knew that because she'd been watching it and wait-

ing for her chance. Apparently, she wasn't about to get one
just yet.

"What's your name?" he asked.

The question, as well as the conversational tone in his
voice, seemed more than a little peculiar in the situation. In
fact, Kira couldn't help but laugh.

"I guess you're in the habit of riding down strange
women and pulling a gun on them?" she asked. "Or are you
one of those bandits who likes to get to know their victims
before they rob them?"

Taking her unspoken cue, the man reached up and
pulled the mask from his face. He was handsome in a
rugged sort of way with features that looked like smooth
lines worn into the side of a rock.

"I'm not a bandit. My name's Clint Adams."

"And I'm Kira Vallejo, but I suppose you already knew
that."

"Yeah. I did. Things tend to go a little smoother once
folks introduce themselves, that's all."

"How very civil of you. Maybe now you can put that
gun away."

Clint shook his head. "Besides your name, I also know
you're a dangerous woman. I want you to take this," he said
while grabbing some rope hanging from his saddle and
tossing it to her. "Tie a knot around your ankles and then
I'll put the gun away."

Kira bent at the knees to pick up the rope. When she
looked up at him, Clint could see the trouble brewing in
her eyes. Even with that bit of warning, he wasn't fully
prepared for what came next.

She charged him like an angry bull, completely ignoring the pistol in his hand.

TWENTY-THREE

Clint might have expected a move like this from a wild-eyed cowboy. He might have even expected to be attacked by a drunk. But the fact that Kira was a woman didn't even have much to do with it. Charging him straight on the way she did was just plain crazy.

Even so, she did a hell of a job.

With her head down and arms outstretched, she dug her boots into the sand and came at him like she meant to push him all the way into California. Since he was caught somewhat off his guard, Clint didn't have time to do much. Whatever time he might have had was wasted with him trying to think of a way to stop her without hurting her.

Kira hit him square in the gut. Clint's reflex was to tense his muscles, which caused her to bounce against him without doing any damage. Her next move wasn't so hard to guess, especially considering why she was running in the first place.

"Oh, no, you don't," Clint said as he twisted his hips and lifted one leg to block the incoming kick to his groin.

Her knee bounced off his with an impressive amount of force. Before her foot even made it back down, she was straightening up and swiping at his face with her fingers.

Clint leaned back, but was unable to avoid the swipe completely. A few of her nails ripped through his cheek, drawing some blood, but not enough to worry about. Rather than let her have another couple swings at him, Clint reached out with his left hand to push flat against the upper portion of her chest.

His palm slapped just beneath her neck and just above her breasts, allowing him to push her back without much fuss. "There's no need for all of th—" His words were cut short by a quick jab to his chin.

Since he'd been in the middle of talking when he caught the punch, Clint felt his teeth rattle together. That noise filled his head and sent a stinging pain through his jaw. The next thing he felt was Kira's hands trying to yank the Colt from his grasp.

Gritting his teeth, Clint leaned forward and closed the hand that was still against her upper body. He managed to get a decent handful of her shirt collar, which was exactly what he'd been after. While holding his right arm back as far as he could, he pulled Kira off balance enough for him to lift her up and back with a slight shove from his left arm.

Kira had still been trying to get Clint's gun from him when she'd been pulled forward. When she felt herself swept back again, her eyes widened and she struggled to keep her balance. Before she knew what was going on, the sky and ground switched places and she was on her way down. Her back slammed against the sand with a solid thump. If that had been rock or even packed dirt beneath her, she might have been knocked out altogether.

Keeping his left hand in place, Clint held her down as he settled on top of her. "I was just about to say that there's no need for this."

"You're trying to kill me," she said viciously.

"I already told you that's not true."

"Then what's the meaning of this? Let me go!"

Clint managed to kneel on top of her. It took a bit of doing, but he also got her arms pinned down beneath his knees. Only then did he holster the Colt. Rubbing at his jaw with his free hand, Clint smirked and said, "You've got a lot of nerve acting so high-and-mighty. Don't you remember blasting your way out of Taloosa?"

Kira stared up at him defiantly. Her dark eyes and thin nose made her face look angular and sharp. Even the scowl she wore couldn't make her mouth look any less attractive, however. Her lips were full, and appeared to be an even darker shade of red when compared to the fiery color of her hair.

"I remember what I did," she replied. "None of that has a damn thing to do with you."

"On the contrary. It's got plenty to do with me since I'm the one that's bringing you in."

The anger on her face deepened and her cheeks flushed to an even brighter red. "You're not bringing me anywhere," she said.

"That's some pretty tough talk coming from a lady in your position."

Suddenly, Kira squirmed with an amount of strength that nearly caught Clint by surprise. It might have caught him completely off guard if he hadn't already seen what she was capable of for himself.

She managed to pull one arm free, simply because the sand underneath it was looser than the rest. When she twisted her body, Kira used nearly every muscle she had to try and get free from underneath Clint. She had plenty of room to wriggle between his legs, but his other knee was now pressing down on her wrist hard enough to numb it.

Clint tried a couple times to get ahold of her free hand, but it was like trying to catch a tadpole while it was still in the water. Her hips twisted one way and then another before her hand came straight up to take a swing at his face. Since he'd been waiting for that move to come, Clint

ducked the swing with ease and grabbed her arm before
she could pull it back again.

Somehow, Kira had gotten onto her side and she was
looking up at Clint with a fire in her eyes. "Let me go," she
growled.

"You're not . . . going anywhere," Clint said while also
trying to pin her down again. And just as he started forcing
her wrist back to the ground, Clint felt her other arm pop
free from underneath his knee.

Rather than try to hold her down the same way he had
before, Clint shot both his legs back so he could use his
hands a little easier. Fortunately for him, it was his right
hand that now needed to get a hold of Kira's wrist. With
the speed that he might pull his Colt from its holster, Clint
snapped his arm forward and locked a firm grip around
Kira's wrist.

For a moment, she looked stunned that she'd been cap-
tured so quickly. Then, once Clint leaned forward and
pushed both of her wrists to the ground, her expression
shifted to something very different.

Both of Kira's wrists were immobilized and pinned to
the sand on either side of her head. Clint was still on top of
her, but he was now leaning down so that his face was only
a foot or so away from hers.

"You're hurting me," she said.

"And you already punched me in the jaw, scratched my
face, and tried to knee me in the groin. I'd say I'm still well
ahead where hurting is concerned."

With her breaths running swiftly through her chest and
her blood racing through her veins, Kira squirmed a bit
more against Clint's body. She could feel his muscles
tensed against her. The more strength he used to hold her
down, the more Kira found herself enjoying the struggle.

Clint was breathing heavily as well. He also recognized
the hungry look that was starting to show on her face.

When Kira breathed in, her eyes widened a little bit. When she breathed out, the traces of a grin showed at the corners of her lips.

"So what are you going to do to me now?" she asked.

Clint had plenty of ideas. Before he could answer the question, however, he heard the rumble of hooves beating against the packed sand. Kira must have heard it as well, since her head turned at the same time as Clint's when he looked in the direction of that sound.

"How many men were coming after you?" Clint asked.

"Including you . . . two."

"Well, it sounds like more than one other rider is headed this way."

"Maybe they're not after me."

One shot cracked through the air to punch up a mound of dirt several paces from Clint and Kira. Another shot followed soon after it.

Keeping a tight grip on Kira's wrists, Clint hauled her to her feet and said, "There goes that theory."

TWENTY-FOUR

The shots were coming closer and closer together as the other riders approached. Kira was snapping her head back and forth to try and look around Eclipse so she could get a look at what was coming for her.

"What are you doing?" she screamed when she felt the rope bite into her wrists and draw tight.

While she'd been distracted, Clint had taken the opportunity to tie a quick loop around her wrists. It was a move that would have made any cowboy proud. "Getting you ready to ride," he said. "That's what I'm doing."

"I can't ride with my hands tied!"

"And you can't get away from me too easily also. Just shut up and get onto your horse."

"How the hell am I supposed to—" Before she could finish her question, Kira was lifted off her feet and tossed over Clint's shoulder like a sack of potatoes. Just as she was starting to kick, she was draped over the back of her horse.

Clint took her reins and climbed onto Eclipse's back.

"I'm just going to fall off," she screamed.

"Then you'd better hang on. And if you're thinking about taking your chances," he added, "just remember that the odds are you'll land on your head if you try to kick off of there."

Even though Clint didn't have the first clue as to what the odds were when it came to flopping off a horse's back, he could tell that he'd given Kira something to think about. That was good enough, so he snapped his reins and brought her horse right along with him.

The moment she felt her horse start to move, Kira let out a shriek through gritted teeth. Her body went stiff as she did her best to maintain her balance. Her eyes were clenched shut and both hands were clenched into tight fists.

Clint only took her less than twenty yards. That was just enough to get her horse behind Eclipse while he drew the rifle from its scabbard on the saddle. Sighting along the rifle's barrel, Clint picked out three targets thundering toward them. He ignored the gunshots crackling through the air, took careful aim, and pulled his trigger.

One of the horses in the distance let out a whinny and kicked up its front legs.

Nodding quickly to himself, Clint levered in the next round and took another shot. This bullet also found its mark and almost knocked one of the men from their saddle. He worked the lever again and fired. This time, he only needed to get the shot close to the remaining rider to show him the error of his ways. After that, all three of them split off in opposite directions.

"They're going to kill you and then me," Kira said. "Is that what you want?"

"They're gone."

"Really?"

"Take a look for yourself," Clint said.

Since she was draped over her horse and facing the wrong direction, there was no way for Kira's body to bend enough for her to get a look at the three retreating riders. Instead, she glared at Clint and said, "Very funny. Are you going to untie me now?"

Clint laughed and reloaded the rifle. "Sure. I'll just untie you and hand back your gun. How about I turn my back on you, close my eyes, and count to ten while I'm at it?"

Kira's lips were pressed together into a thin line. Her eyes were nearly pinched shut as she stared daggers through Clint's face. "You're real funny, mister."

"I told you, my name's Clint."

"Sorry, but I didn't think to address my kidnapper by his proper name."

"You still think this is a kidnapping?"

"What would you call it?"

"How about a capture?" Clint said. "Or chasing down a wanted fugitive?"

Although the petulant look on Kira's face remained, she didn't say anything else. At least, not for the moment. Clint could tell there was plenty boiling just beneath her surface, but decided to enjoy the peace and quiet while it lasted.

"I doubt that's all of the men that will be coming after you," he said. "Do you know anyplace we can go so we can rest up and get ourselves squared away?"

Kira remained quiet. This time, however, she made a show of twisting her head so she was facing as far away from Clint as she could possibly manage.

"Your leg is bleeding."

She glanced toward her left side, shifted a bit, but didn't speak.

"We should probably get a look at that before we move on. This isn't the place you want to be hurt."

"Too late for that, mister."

Clint moved closer to her and leaned over so he could almost see her face. Before too long, she peeked to see what he was doing and found Clint staring straight down at her. Rather than twist away again, she stared right back.

"Where were you headed before?" he asked. "We need someplace those men won't find us." When he saw there was no answer coming, he added, "They're probably doubling back right now. This time, they'll probably circle around to hit us from every angle at once."

Still nothing.

"All right then," Clint said after letting out a measured breath. "Answer this for me. Would you rather be with me and put up with some awkward conversation, or would you rather be with those bounty hunters, who are probably still deciding whether you would be worth more turned in to the law, sold to some Indians, or just kept around so they can have you all to themselves?"

"Keep heading northwest," she said after a few seconds. "I'll tell you where to go from there."

Clint took hold of Kira's reins and got Eclipse's nose pointed in the right direction. "There now, that wasn't so hard."

Kira kept quiet and held onto whatever part of the saddle she could grab.

TWENTY-FIVE

The spot Kira directed Clint to wasn't exactly an oasis, but it was the next best thing. Since he couldn't ride at full speed for fear of allowing Kira to be dumped somewhere along the way, Clint spent the better part of the day riding in silence. Every now and then, he would receive a shouted instruction or two from the redhead, but he eventually didn't need any more of her grunted words to go by.

He spotted the town from a few miles away. It stuck out like a sore thumb since it had been built on a flat bed of sandy rock in the middle of nowhere. For some places, that was just an expression. For this one, it couldn't have been more literal if the word "nowhere" was actually written on a map and this place was smack in the center of it.

It was a small town, consisting of only a few buildings that were tall enough to show up on the horizon. As Clint rode closer, he saw that there were several other buildings here and there in the town. The only problem was that they'd been knocked down or blown over some time ago.

As far as Clint could tell, there hadn't been anyone living in that town for at least a few years. And when the residents had picked up and gone away, they'd done so in a rush. Like Taloosa, there were a few houses scattered here and there outside the town itself. Those were in fairly good condition, and one still even had curtains in the windows.

After riding past those houses, Clint found himself in the town itself. The streets were flooded with sand, making it hard to tell if the boardwalk was raised or just rows of wooden planks set into the ground. There was only one main street and a smaller cross street. The storefronts were like wooden skeletons lined up in a ghost of a town.

"I think this used to be a copper town," Kira said. "Either that or maybe silver."

"How long's it been deserted?"

"I don't know. I found it when I was out for a ride."

Clint looked over at her and asked, "Did you often just strike out across the desert for a ride?"

Without looking at him, she replied, "Yes." Her voice was tired and she drooped over the side of her horse like there was no more life in her body.

Throughout the ride, Clint had noticed the ropes that he'd wrapped around Kira loosening due to the heat and her constant motion. He didn't tighten them simply so he could see what she would do. If she was going to try and escape, he knew he could easily pick her up again. If she was going to be civil, perhaps he could extend her the same courtesy. Of course, there was always the possibility that she would do neither of those things.

She could just be a smart woman biding her time.

Unfortunately, Clint wasn't having as much luck reading her face as he might in deciding whether or not someone was bluffing at the card table. It seemed that Kira was well versed in putting up a brick wall and keeping it up.

"Any suggestions on where we should stay?" he asked.

She picked that moment to shut her mouth again.

"Fine," Clint said as he craned his neck and took a look around.

Although there were several buildings that were more or

less in one piece, a few of them had obviously become home to animals. There was one building in particular that caught his eye, simply because most of the windows seemed to be intact. When he saw the letters painted across the window, Clint smiled.

"How about that one?" he asked.

She lifted her head to get a look at which one he was talking about. The paint on the windows was chipped and faded, but there was enough for her to see the little structure used to be a bank. "Doesn't matter," she grunted. "I don't care."

Clint brought Eclipse to a stop and jumped from the saddle. He pushed open the front door, took a look inside, and smiled again. "This is just as good as I thought it would be," he said. "Looks like we've found ourselves a room for the night."

Soon, Clint was walking back into the bank. This time, however, he had Kira slung over his shoulder. He could feel her shifting within the loose ropes, but that was about all the movements she made. She didn't even bother looking around as he carried her inside.

The front of the bank was just big enough to hold four or five people cramped together. A dividing wall cut all the way across the room, sectioned off by two teller's windows and a narrow door that was missing its handle. That door came open without a hitch, allowing Clint to move around behind the wall.

Back there, most of the space was taken up by a few large desks and a medium-sized safe that looked as if it had been through a war. The sides and top were scorched, the floor beneath it was cracked, and the door was hanging off half a hinge.

"Looks like someone's already been through the good stuff," Clint said. "That means there's no reason for anyone to bother us."

Kira grunted and said, "Being carried off by those bounty hunters is sounding better and better."

"Oh, that's just the heat talking. I'm sure you'll feel better once I get those ropes off of you."

Her eyes widened and a smile jumped onto her face. "You're going to untie me?"

"Sure. First, I want you to see if you can slip your hands out from between the ropes."

She went through a few squirms, and then finally her hands emerged from between the ropes that had been wrapped around her.

Clint loosened the end of the rope that had knotted the whole mess together and quickly looped that end around her wrists. Before Kira had time to protest, she felt the ropes cinch in yet again around her wrists.

"I knew I shouldn't listen to a thing you say," she grumbled.

Shaking his head, Clint continued untying her until the only thing that was bound by ropes was her wrists. "There now," he said. "Isn't that better?"

"I guess you'll want my ankles next?"

Clint was already up and walking toward the dividing wall. Reaching out to one of the teller's windows, he took hold of the iron grate that filled in most of the opening. He pulled on the grate and felt it wobble within its frame. The second one didn't so much as budge, however, so that was the spot where he tied the free end of the rope.

"It may not be a fancy hotel," he said, "but I'll wager it beats the hell out of the back of your horse."

Slowly, Kira's expression softened. She even began to nod as she said, "Yes, I suppose it does."

"Now, I just need to find somewhere to put the horses. Will you be all right here for a little bit?"

She nodded quickly. Actually, she nodded a little too quickly.

Narrowing his eyes a bit, Clint drew his Colt and held it

down at his side. "Put your hands up and turn around," he said.

Kira rolled her eyes, but complied.

When she turned in a slow circle with her arms held high, Kira's hips shifted invitingly back and forth. Her dusty jeans clung to her figure in a way that accentuated every last curve. Sections of her shirt were ripped, exposing the smooth skin underneath.

Clint stepped up and used his free hand to feel up and down along her sides. Even though his intention was to check her pockets and to make sure she wasn't hiding anything she could use to escape, he couldn't help but enjoy his job. Her body was firm, warm, and moved slightly under his touch. Her dark red hair hung over her shoulder, one of which was bare due to a rip in her shirt.

Even though he tried to keep his mind focused on the job at hand, Clint found his thoughts drifting to those fleeting glimpses of bare skin. His fingers brushed against that skin, giving him a taste of what the rest of her body might feel like. When he reached around to feel her front pockets as well as the waistband of her jeans, Clint felt Kira arch slightly against him.

She pulled in a breath, but quickly tensed as though she'd been caught doing something she wasn't supposed to be doing. The lower curve of her breasts brushed against the back of Clint's hand. When he tried to move his hand away, he merely brushed it against the tight curve of her belly.

Clint stepped back and almost left right then and there. He stopped short, since he realized there was one more spot to check. "Your boots," he said. "Kick them off."

Kira lowered her arms, eased herself down onto the floor, and pulled off her boots. With an impatient frown on her face, she turned them over and shook them. The only thing to fall out was a trickle of sand.

Doing his best to keep his voice strong and level, he

said, "I'll be right back. If you make me hunt you down again, just remember you're worth the same dead as alive."

When he stepped out of that bank, the desert heat felt like a splash of cool water.

TWENTY-SIX

After spending so much time in the desert, Clint no longer thought of nighttime as solely a time for sleep. Being the coolest part of the day, the night was a good time to cover a lot of ground. It was easier on himself as well as Eclipse. Even so, that didn't mean he was wide awake after the sun went down. He was merely on his toes.

Kira, on the other hand, showed how much longer she'd been in the desert by the way she came alive as the shadows grew longer. She'd found a comfortable spot with her back against the dividing wall, so there was enough slack in the rope for her to move fairly normally. She seemed in even better spirits once Clint fixed up some dinner.

"Hope you like rabbit," he said. "That's about all I've been able to find."

"Sounds great," she said with an easy smile. "You seem like a hell of a cook."

"With a stove like this, I can't go too wrong." When he said that, Clint motioned over to the old broken-down safe.

The few shelves inside the iron box had been pulled out, leaving it wide-open and empty. Clint had piled up some wood and leaves in there, tossed in a match, and had a nice little blaze going inside. Although the smoke poured out to swirl in the room, the flames were hidden from sight and weren't about to burn the whole town to ashes.

The rabbit Clint had shot outside that little cave was long gone. He'd collected a few others along the way, shooting them when he could and carrying the carcasses in a bundle tied to his saddle. One of those carcasses was on a stick and being cooked, filling the bank with a mouth-watering scent.

Sitting on the floor and shifting the rabbit over the fire, Clint said, "You don't strike me as the sort who would shoot a man."

"I'm not."

"I think there's a few souls in Taloosa who would have something to say about that."

Cringing, Kira drew up her legs so she could wrap her arms around them. She set her chin down on her knees and stared into the strange campfire. "I never thought I could do such a thing. But there's only so many times I could sit back and let Earl put his hands on me after a night of drinking or say nothing when he gambled away what few cents we'd managed to scrape together."

"You could have left, you know."

"I know. Part of me just got comfortable, I guess. Part of me thought I could change him."

Clint let out a grumbling laugh and shook his head. "Jesus. If I had a dollar every time I heard a woman say that about a man . . ."

"I know, I know. It sounds so stupid when I say it out loud. Actually, I was set to leave a few times, but there just wasn't anywhere else to go. Then he asked me to marry him and I thought he actually was starting to change. Guess that was wrong."

"So, what brought you from unhappy to shooting him in the . . . ?" Rather than finish the question, Clint was more inclined to let it hang.

Judging by the smile on her face, Kira was well aware

of his discomfort. "Earl went to a few whores. I knew it. Maybe every man does the same. But when he not only shared that whore's bed, but roughed her up as well, I just couldn't take it anymore.

"He'd been treating me badly enough, but at least there were some good times. Now, he was being a filthy bastard to me as well as to any other woman he could get his hands on." Kira seemed to be staring right into the heart of the fire as she continued her story. "He'd go on hurting more women and because I knew what he was capable of, I was the one who needed to put an end to it. I thought about killing him, but this just seemed more suitable. You know, letting the punishment fit the crime and all that."

Suddenly, Kira snapped her eyes from the fire and looked at Clint. "Do you know if Earl's still alive?"

"Last time I heard, he was alive. The doctor got to him and stitched him up. Of course, I'm not too familiar with how well a man can heal from a wound like that. If you ask him, I bet Earl would wish you had put him down for good."

Kira's eyes narrowed again, and she shifted them back toward the fire. "That whore wasn't the first one he fucked. I found out he put his dick into anything he could, including a few of our neighbors. And after all that, he still had the nerve to nearly kill me every month or two."

She shook her head and said, "He'd get this crazy look in his eyes and jump at me. I can defend myself pretty good, but there's only so much I could do short of . . . well . . . what I finally wound up doing."

Clint's first impulse was to be suspicious of anything that came out of Kira's mouth. Even though he knew better than to take her completely at face value, he tended to believe what she was saying about Earl. Clint knew what she meant regarding that crazy look in his eyes. He'd seen it for himself in Lillian's room. After seeing the man in that state, it wasn't hard to imagine him doing every last thing Kira described.

"I planned it all out," she said as if she was musing over a dream. "At least, I thought I did. I planned out what I would do. I got a gun. I practiced using it. I even planned out where I would go."

"You just forgot to pack a bag for the trip," Clint said.

"That's right! How'd you know about that?"

"Because that's how I picked up your trail. I'd guess that's how those others picked up on it as well. I spotted a horse riding like hell back toward Taloosa. I almost let you go, but then I saw it was a woman in the saddle. After a while, I managed to get a close enough look to see your face and couldn't believe my luck."

She shook her head as though she was embarrassed. "I got all that way and didn't have any clothes or even any money. I figured, since everyone saw me leave town like that, they wouldn't expect me to sneak back in. I don't even know where those other men came from."

"They're out for the bounty. They probably just got started looking when you rode right past them."

"I always did have bad luck with men," she said.

Both of them laughed at the joke as Clint turned the rabbit over the fire.

TWENTY-SEVEN

The rabbit meat was tough and greasy, but it tasted like a feast compared to all the sand that had blown down Clint and Kira's mouths throughout the day. They washed it down with some coffee before Clint set down his cup and stood up so he could walk over to her.

"That was a great meal," Kira said. "How about tomorrow you fix me a nice, thick steak?"

After collecting her dishes, Clint took hold of the long end of rope dangling through the teller's window and over the counter. "Put your ankles together," he said.

"All right, no need to get nasty. Rabbit will be just fine."

"I'm going to have a look around outside," Clint explained. "I'm going to have to make certain you don't go anywhere as well."

"I'm too full to go anywhere."

"Humor me."

Scooting down a little so her back was slouched, Kira kept her eyes on Clint as she stretched out her legs. She scraped her heels slowly against the dirty floor until she could inch them together. "That good enough?" she asked.

"Perfect."

Clint took the other end of the rope and knelt down beside her ankles. After making a few loops around them, he tied a quick knot and said, "Now sit forward and lift your arms."

"This is an awful lot of trouble for nothing. Where would I possibly go?"

Clint stared at her intently and made it clear that he wasn't about to budge until his orders were carried out. Finally, Kira let out a sigh and held her arms up while leaning forward. The exasperated look on her face slowly changed into something that was much more amused when she saw Clint move forward and reach behind her to take out the rope's slack and drop it once more through the teller's window.

Kira even leaned forward a bit more when Clint was close enough for her to brush her cheek against his neck.

"That won't get you anywhere," Clint forced himself to say.

"Maybe it's not for your benefit," she whispered. Her words felt hot against Clint's neck and her lips sent a chill through him as they fluttered against his skin.

Before Clint could say another word, he felt his hat get knocked off his head and Kira's arms drop down on either side. She had to lean forward to make sure the ropes binding her wrists made it over and she wound up having room to spare.

Clint's first reaction was to go for his Colt. He didn't draw the weapon, but he clamped his hand down over it to make sure that she couldn't get to it either. But Kira wasn't a bit concerned with the Colt. Her arms tightened around him and her lips were quick to find Clint's mouth.

The first kiss was fast and somewhat awkward, but that was mostly due to the positioning of both participants. After they'd both shifted their heads a little, the next kiss landed nicely indeed. Kira's lips were smooth and urgently pressed against Clint's. When they leaned in for the third kiss, she opened her mouth so her tongue could dart out and flick over Clint's lips.

Clint responded in kind by parting his own lips. Kira's tongue slid into his mouth and her entire body trembled. With his right hand still on his Colt, Clint slid his left along the side of her body. He started at her waist and then worked his way up over her ribs. He lingered at her breasts so he could feel the warm softness of them before moving all the way up along her arm. By the time he reached her hand, he could hear Kira gasping for her next breath.

She moved her hands up and down along his back, massaging his shoulders while tracing the lines of his muscles. There'd been enough space between her wrists for her to eat and move around well enough. Therefore, there was enough slack for her to get one hand around so she could feel his side and start pulling his shirt from where it had been tucked in. Once she got Clint's shirt untucked, she used that hand to begin pulling at his belt buckle.

He moved her hand away quickly so he could get back to what he was doing. When he felt her hand work its way down the side of his pants, Clint shifted once more.

"If you're so worried about me misbehaving," she whispered, "put that gun somewhere I can't get to it."

Clint thought about it for close to two seconds. The fact of the matter was that he'd made up his mind after less than one of those seconds had passed.

TWENTY-EIGHT

Clint's gun belt lay coiled up and wedged partly under the broken safe. With the floor underneath the safe so busted up, it was easy for him to jam the belt under the safe so that the gun was held firmly inside. Since that placed his gun safely on the other side of the room and nowhere near a door, Clint could concentrate on more interesting things.

Kira lay against the dividing wall with her hands over her head and the end of the rope looped around the cage of the teller's window. She wasn't being held in that position by the rope. On the contrary, she seemed to have taken a liking to it all on her own. One of her legs was stretched out, while the other was bent at the knee so her foot could lie flat upon the floor.

Her clothes were rumpled and one of her ponytails had come loose. Her eyes watched Clint's every move, and a naughty little smile made her lips all the more inviting.

"Sure you don't want to tie me up a little tighter?" she asked. "After all, I may just get away from you."

Clint had already kicked off his boots and was climbing down to settle on top of her. Both hands were now free to roam up and down over her body and he took his time to

112

sample every one of her curves. "Then I'll just have to keep you real close," he said.

The moment she felt his hands work their way onto her breasts, Kira arched her back and let out an anxious moan. She couldn't keep her arms where they were for one more second, so she dropped them down once more over Clint's head.

It was a little awkward having her wrists bound by that length of rope, but it also added to their game. As Clint ducked, Kira pulled her arms back so she could use her hands to pull open Clint's shirt. He returned the favor by unbuttoning hers all the way down. Instead of trying to get it off her, Clint just moved on to the next set of buckles and fasteners, which held her jeans shut.

By the time Clint had her belt off and jeans loosened, Kira was practically squirming out of them. Clint took a few moments to hook both hands under her waistband so he could peel the denim off her to reveal the smooth slope of her hips and the tight muscles of her thighs.

Kira kicked the jeans off the moment she could, and then opened her legs so Clint could crawl between them. Rather than try to only use one hand at a time, she kept both of them on his shoulders and chest. Her hips moved more than enough to make Clint forget about the rope entirely. The more she rubbed herself against his growing erection, the wetter she got between her own legs.

Clint pushed his hands underneath Kira's shirt so he could cup her breasts. They were just enough to fill his hands, and he could feel her nipples becoming hard with just a few quick rubs. She closed her eyes and leaned her head back to savor the way he touched her. When she spoke, Kira's voice was soft and breathy.

"I want you inside me," she whispered. "Now."

All Clint needed to do was shift his hips a bit and he felt the tip of his cock sliding between the lips of her pussy.

Kira spread her legs open a bit wider for him and waited anxiously. She didn't have to wait long before his rigid penis was slipping inside her.

"Oh, my God," she breathed.

Clint grabbed hold of her legs beneath her knees so he could pump in and out of her freely. Soon, they began to knock against the dividing wall hard enough to send an echo through the mostly empty bank. Both of them stopped and grinned at each other like a couple of kids in their teens trying not to get caught in a loft.

"I don't think this is going to work," Kira said regretfully.

"Nonsense," Clint replied. "Just hang onto me."

Without another word, Clint stood up and brought Kira right along with him. She quickly looped her arms around his neck and used her legs to steady herself the moment she could get them under her. She wore an excited smile as Clint put his hands under her arms and lifted her onto the counter of the dividing wall where the bank tellers would have counted out their change.

The narrow counter creaked a bit at first, but was strong enough to support Kira's weight. Once she was certain she wasn't about to fall, Kira wrapped her legs around Clint's waist and pulled him closer to her. In another second, he was entering her once more.

Clint used both hands to cup her firm, rounded backside as he thrust in and out of her. Still enjoying the ropes around her wrists, Kira reached up and grabbed hold of the upper portion of the teller's cage. That caused her back to arch beautifully, causing her breasts to emerge from her unbuttoned shirt.

Every time Clint pumped forward, she arched her back and sucked in a deep breath. Kira's legs were spread wide open and her head was turned to one side. Soon, she let out little grunts every time Clint's body slapped against hers.

The warmth of her skin melted into Clint's hands. She was so wet between her legs that he glided in and out of her with ease. The harder he pounded into her, the louder Kira moaned. When he pounded into her as hard as he could, she arched her back and shouted his name.

Just as she was starting to tremble with her second climax, Kira felt the counter start to give way beneath her. Clint felt it too, but didn't stop what he was doing. Instead, he grabbed onto her buttocks more firmly, and when the counter did crack and give way, he was more than able to hold her up.

They looked down at the crumbling counter and let out a few laughs. All Kira had to do was lower one leg and she was able to stand on her own. The other leg stayed around Clint's waist, allowing her to wriggle her hips in time to his thrusts.

From this new angle, Clint's penis rubbed against a spot in Kira's body that took her breath away. She tightened her grip around the back of his neck while grinding against him and whispering into his ear.

"That's it, Clint. Right there. Oh, I'm going to . . ."

She was unable to finish her sentence because every muscle in her body clenched as intense pleasure spiked along every inch of her flesh.

Clint had one hand pressed against the small of Kira's back and the other tightly gripping her backside. With that grip, he was able to pull her closer while he buried himself inside her again and again. Although Kira was trying to speak, all he could hear was breathless moans. Even so, the heat of her breath on his neck was enough to send a special chill down his spine.

With a few more powerful strokes, Clint pressed Kira up against the dividing wall. Her body was trembling and she was gasping for breath by the time he finally exploded inside her. He stood there for as long as he could, but soon his legs began to weaken.

The moment his grip loosened, Kira eased away from Clint and slid down the dividing wall. She sat with her legs

drawn into her body and didn't bother closing her shirt. Instead, she looked at Clint with hungry eyes as a few trick-
les of sweat moved down her neck and between her breasts.

"I think I'm starting to really like these ropes," she said.

"Good, because you're staying in them while I have a
look around this town."

Before Kira could work her pouting lip too much, Clint
handed her a blanket. "Sit tight and try to get some sleep.
I'll be back before too long."

TWENTY-NINE

For the most part, the town was similar to a buffalo's carcass that had been picked clean and laid out to bleach in the sun. Even with just the pale moonlight to go by, Clint could tell that all of the paint had flaked off and blown away from the walls that were exposed to the elements. Doors hung on broken hinges and shutters rattled like broken teeth hanging from a set of poorly tended gums.

The first place Clint went was across the street to some of the closest storefronts. As far as he could tell, they were the remains of a barbershop, a store, and probably some sort of restaurant. Naturally, there wasn't anything on the shelves or behind the counters. Even the walls were falling apart.

A bit further down the street was a saloon. Clint could tell that much by the heap of a bar that still stood on one side of the main room. Since that room was large and the walls were fairly intact, Clint led the horses into it and tied them to a section of the bar. A pump outside was rusted pretty badly, but a few minutes of hard work got the handle moving and a trickle of water flowing. It wasn't much, but it was enough to satisfy the horses for the time being.

"Don't worry, you two," Clint said while patting both

animals on the necks. "I'll come back with some more. I'll also see about finding something for you to eat. There's got to be something for you around here."

"After that, how about you fix me a drink?"

The instant Clint heard that voice, he turned on the balls of his feet and drew the Colt from its holster. "I was wondering if you were going to make the first move or if I would have to hunt you down."

The other man stood just inside the doorway with both hands held at shoulder height. An amused expression was on his sunken face, causing the top of his drooping mustache to bend upward. His voice sounded as if it had been raked over rough slate for three weeks on end. "Oh, you knew I was here? I suppose this was all just some clever trap then."

"I knew you were here as of a minute ago," Clint replied. "With the condition this town is in, it's not hard to spot fresh tracks in the street."

"I guess you got me there. Can I put my hands down, or were you planning on shooting me?"

"You can do what you like. Just know that if you twitch toward those guns of yours, I'll have to shoot you anyway."

The stranger wore a double-rig holster around his waist and carried twin .44's in it. Glancing down at those guns, the man said, "Fair enough. I only came here to have a word with you anyhow."

"Then have your word," Clint said while turning some of his attention back to Eclipse. "I'm listening."

Taking a cautious step into the saloon, the man asked, "Are you really Clint Adams?"

"Last time I checked."

"Why would a man like you be going after a bitch like Kira Vallejo?"

"That's an odd question. Especially since I'd wager you're after that same woman."

"I am, but that's my business."

"So you're a bounty hunter?"

He nodded. "Don McKay. You ever hear the name?"

"Can't say as I have."

McKay winced as if he'd been rapped on the nose. "Surely you're not in need of that bounty. From what I've heard, you can make up that amount of money in a few card games. You play with the heavy hitters, so why not let some of us little fish have this one?"

Now that both horses were squared away for the night, Clint put his back to them and started walking straight toward McKay. He didn't say a word as he walked. Instead, he watched the other man carefully to see how he would react.

If McKay had bad intentions, he would probably act on them the moment he felt like he was cornered. If he was truly there to talk, then he would probably just keep talking.

Clint made it all the way to within a few feet of McKay without the bounty hunter doing more than taking half a step back. "Were those your men that tried to gun us down when we were riding yesterday?" Clint asked.

"No."

"Would you tell me if they were?"

McKay started to reply, but stopped himself. He cocked his head slightly and showed Clint a devious smile. "That's one of those questions that can't be answered right. You think I'm here to cause trouble?"

"I was shot at not too long ago and expect that I'll be shot at again. Along comes Don McKay and I'm supposed to just rejoice and welcome him with open arms? For all I know, you just came here so you could take what you wanted and leave me in the desert to rot."

"I wasn't thinking anything of the sort."

Clint stepped past him so he could get outside. Standing in the doorway so he could see McKay as well as the street, Clint asked, "What is it you're after?"

"Just thought I'd ask if you needed any help bringing this woman in."

"And why would I need any help?"

"This is an unforgiving stretch of land. It's filled with some rough characters, some of which you've already met. Since it's too late for me to find that . . . woman, then maybe I could be of some assistance in bringing her in."

Clint's eyes narrowed as he studied McKay. Normally, he trusted his instincts when judging the intentions of others. This time, however, he didn't quite know what to make of the man in his sights.

"What if I refuse?" Clint asked.

"Then I guess I'd leave."

Clint stepped to one side and held the door open. With his other hand, he made a sweeping gesture as if clearing the path for royalty to pass in front of him.

With nothing more than a shrug, McKay left.

THIRTY

Clint stood and watched as McKay got onto his horse and rode away. The bounty hunter even threw a friendly wave over his shoulder before snapping his reins and leaving town. Although Clint wasn't sure about McKay's true intentions, he was fairly certain he'd be seeing the man again. In fact, he thought he'd be seeing him very soon indeed.

After going back into the saloon so he could collect his rifle and saddlebag, he carried them to the barbershop across the street from the bank and set them inside the door. He then led both horses to that same shop, and repeated the process of getting the animals situated for the night. The shop wasn't nearly as spacious as the saloon, but he could keep an eye on that place much easier since it was so close to the bank.

As far as that bank was concerned, Clint hadn't so much as looked at it since McKay had left. Instead, he came and went from the barbershop so many times that his steps cleared off a clean path through the dust that had collected upon the boards outside the shop's front door. He even went so far as to create a spot in the front corner of the shop where he could build a small fire. It was well away from the horses, would keep them warm, and would have been big enough to cook up a decent meal.

Once he'd gotten the fire going and was certain the flames weren't about to spread, Clint attached a leather strap to the rifle and slung it across his back. He patted the horses one more time as he walked past them, eased open one of the windows at the back of the shop, and crawled outside.

Clint hunkered down and stayed still as soon as his boots hit the dirt. Although his eyes were searching every shadow he could find, he paid more attention to what little bits and pieces his ears could gather.

Like most desert nights, it was quiet enough for him to hear nearly everything that stirred within a quarter of a mile. With the town being completely dead, Clint figured he might be able to hear even further out than that.

If he concentrated, he could hear the occasional clomping of hooves against the shop's floorboards.

He could hear the crackle of the fire.

He could hear the rustle of the wind.

That was it.

Satisfied, Clint stayed low and hurried to the neighboring building. That one was in much worse shape than the barbershop, which meant it was awfully close to collapsing in on itself. Using the loose boards and crooked gutters to his advantage, Clint climbed up the corner of the building that was sloped down the most. He worked his way carefully across the roof toward the front of the structure where he could look down on a good section of the entire town.

More than once, pieces of the roof shifted and creaked beneath Clint's boots. Thanks to some quick reflexes and quicker footwork, Clint managed to stretch out on his belly, take the rifle from where it had been slung, and get situated without collapsing the roof. A few chunks of wood dropped inside the shop, but that didn't make enough noise to distinguish itself from the rest of the creaks and groans accompanying every passing breeze.

With the skeletal remains of the buildings and the dead quiet of the air, it wasn't hard to see why places like these were called ghost towns. As the wind whistled through broken glass and howled within empty buildings, that name seemed even more fitting.

Clint reached out to rub one hand along the edge of the roof. His fingers were immediately covered with a mix of mold, dirt, and mud, which he then smeared along the barrel of his rifle. That way, when he rested the barrel on the roof, none of the moonlight reflected off the iron. After removing his hat and stuffing it under his leg, Clint figured he was practically invisible to the street below.

With those tasks completed, all that remained was to wait.

The streets were empty.

It looked as though Kira wasn't moving either. After studying what he could through the bank's window, Clint wondered if he should have checked in on her personally to make sure she didn't spoil what he was trying to do. Then again, if he was right, Clint didn't plan on having to wait very long before he got the answers he was after.

About twenty minutes later, he got them.

Clint grinned as he picked out one shadow breaking off from the others to inch along the side of the street. Just as Clint had figured, McKay was sneaking his way right along the tracks that had been so carefully put in place.

THIRTY-ONE

McKay crept through the darkness with the sure steps and confidence of a professional. He kept his body low and his chin up so he could see where he was going while watching his surroundings. Even if he could see in the dark, however, there wasn't much of a chance that he could pick out the set of eyes watching him from above.

Clint's chin was resting on the side of his rifle, but he didn't want to take a shot just yet. Instead, he watched McKay walk all the way down the street until he got to the stretch of abandoned buildings where the bank and barbershop faced each other. Now, Clint would see just how much McKay knew and what he was after.

If McKay had been following Clint for a while, he would know exactly where Kira was being kept, and would probably go there first to make sure his bounty was where it was supposed to be.

If McKay had somehow stumbled across Clint or even guessed he might come across him at the ghost town, then he would have only been watching Clint for a short time. If that was the case, he would think that the barbershop was the spot where Clint was holed up.

McKay didn't so much as glance toward the bank as he

did his best to keep his steps light and quick on his way to the barbershop. If he was strictly an outside observer, Clint would even have to give some credit to the bounty hunter as he was almost as silent as the shadows around him as he crossed the street and worked his way closer to his target.

Easing himself a bit more toward the edge of the roof, Clint was able to keep track of McKay as he moved directly beneath him. Now that the bounty hunter was close enough for Clint to hear him, Clint shifted his eyes to the other parts of town.

He was looking to see if there were any others following along in McKay's wake. There weren't a lot of places for anyone to hide from Clint since he'd gotten a good piece of high ground. If anyone else was trying to sneak around on the streets, they'd have to be smaller than a rat to completely escape Clint's notice.

Just as Clint was about to look back toward McKay, he spotted someone poking their head around a corner at the far end of the street. At first, Clint thought he'd been spotted. But when the figure in the distance took a step out, he wasn't looking up at any of the rooftops.

He was looking at McKay.

The figure didn't make a sound as he raised a hand and pointed toward the bounty hunter. After that signal was given, two more figures emerged from behind one of the buildings at the far end of town. Like the first one, these other two crept like they were born for the job. They were also armed to the teeth since the moonlight glinted off several firearms distributed among all three men.

"Come on," Clint whispered under his breath as he shifted his sights back to McKay. "Turn around."

McKay not only kept moving toward the barbershop without a glance over his shoulder, he seemed completely oblivious to the presence of the other three.

Several different options flooded Clint's mind. Those other three could be with McKay and just following some plan that had been discussed earlier. They could be hanging back to try and get Clint to tip his hand or give away his position. They might even be trying to flush out Kira. Of course, they could also be there to get rid of McKay altogether and continue the hunt on their own.

There was no reason for Clint to feel any loyalty to McKay. He'd never even heard of the man until a few minutes ago. Then again, he wasn't comfortable with sitting back to watch if those other three meant to ambush McKay and kill him on the spot.

The longer Clint watched those other three, the more likely that last possibility seemed. And the more time that passed, the more likely it became for Kira to make a noise and spoil the whole ruse outright. Clint cursed himself for not taking the time to just stick his head into the bank and tell her to keep quiet.

Suddenly, Clint's heart skipped a beat as yet another possibility entered his mind. This one pulled together a lot of different threads and seemed to make plenty of sense. If it was the truth, however, then things might be headed in a very dangerous direction.

But there wasn't any more time for speculation. Those three weren't just closing in on McKay, but they were flanking him to boot. Not only that, but McKay was already close enough to the barbershop to start peeking into windows.

As Clint watched, one of the other three men sidestepped from the walkway in front of the shops so he could slip around the corner. His gun was drawn and he kept himself facing McKay the entire time. Although the man's steps were quiet, he was obviously ready to pull his trigger if McKay decided to look in the wrong direction at the wrong time.

If that man made it around the back of the barbershop, the game would be over. The building was small enough that they'd be able to see there were only horses in there from the back window. Also, they would get McKay trapped in a deadly cross fire with practically no chance of survival.

McKay was peeking in through the barbershop window, making it even clearer to Clint that McKay hadn't been watching him for very long. Although McKay could surely make out the horses inside the shop, there were plenty of dark corners and other spots where Kira could be hiding. Muttering something under his breath. McKay walked toward the corner where that other man was waiting so he could get a look through another window.

Taking quick stock of the situation, Clint saw that the other two men had taken up positions across the street. One of them had the front of the barbershop and the left side in his sights. The other man had the front and right side covered. Between all three of them, there was no way for McKay to make it out of there alive.

After one of the three gunmen nodded, the other one raised a rifle and sighted along its barrel.

Clint had a decision to make, and very little time in which to make it.

THIRTY-TWO

McKay took one more glimpse into the front window of the barbershop. Although the angle was slightly different, the only things he could see in there were a pair of horses' rumps and some saddlebags. The building was only one room, but he couldn't see every last inch of the place. If Clint had seen him coming, he could be hiding in a few places. He could even be hiding directly beneath the front window, which didn't sit well with McKay at all.

The bounty hunter felt a chill run up his spine that had nothing to do with the cool desert night. He could feel eyes on him, which made his hand drift toward his gun. He kept his eyes on that window, waiting for the first sign of movement. Clint had seemed like a friendly enough sort, but that didn't mean McKay was anxious to show him his back.

As his heart pounded heavily in his chest and he waited to see someone pop up in front of him, he heard the rattle of something scraping to his left. That rattle was quickly followed by a grunt, which could only come from a man.

Shifting quickly on the balls of his feet, McKay turned to his left and drew one of his .44's. "Who's there?" he snapped.

Since his cover was already spoiled, the man stepped

out from where he'd been hiding along the side of the barbershop. His face was dirty and covered with scars. His expression could barely pass for a smile. It was more of a twisted curl of his flaking lips.

"Who the hell are you?" McKay asked.

"We was just about to ask the same thing," the man replied.

"We?" With that question still in the air, McKay took a quick look around. He managed to pick out one other shape across the street. Since he didn't want to take his eyes off the first man, he saw the second out of the very edge of his field of vision. "What do you two want?"

The closest man grinned a bit more and took a confident step forward. "We're here for the same reason as you. We're here for the woman."

"Kira Vallejo?"

"That's the one."

"If you're after the bounty, we can work together and split it."

The man in the alley grimaced as if McKay had just suggested unnatural relations with his mother. "Ain't no reason to split anything, asshole. 'Specially now that we know where she is."

"Surely we can work something out."

"You ain't in a spot to make any deals," the filthy man said with a laugh. "But you got our thanks for bringing us here to this spot. It might have taken us an extra hour or two without yer help."

That brought out some laughter from the man across the street. McKay, on the other hand, didn't seem so amused. He took a few steps back so he could keep both men in his sight at the same time. As he moved, his other hand drifted toward the second .44 at his side.

The man that had been doing the talking stepped out of the shadows where he'd been hiding. Although he kept his eyes on McKay, he also kept shooting glances up toward the tops of the surrounding buildings. The more times he looked up there, the tenser he became.

McKay found himself constantly shifting his eyes between the two men. They were standing far enough apart that one of them could always be just out of sight. Even though McKay could keep them both in his line of sight, he could only see them as shadowy blobs. Whenever he looked away from one, he knew the other was getting ready to fire. The more he thought about his odds here, the less he liked them.

Just then, a shot cracked through the air. It didn't come from McKay or either of the other two men. Instead, it came from somewhere above the first man's position and sent a bullet down toward McKay.

The bounty hunter instinctively dropped down and took a shot toward that rooftop. When he heard the grunt coming from behind him, McKay knew he hadn't been the intended target of that shot. Pivoting toward that new voice, the bounty hunter spotted the third gunman positioned across the street.

"Goddamn assassins," McKay snarled as he filled his other hand with the second .44. He pulled his left trigger a few times, throwing lead across the street. He took a bit more time with his right-hand gun since that man was close enough to be a bigger threat.

It wasn't much of a surprise when the street exploded with gunfire coming from every direction. The men across the street from the barbershop ducked behind whatever cover they could find as lead whipped through the air toward them.

"There's another son of a bitch up there!" one of the men across the street shouted while stabbing a finger toward a rooftop.

The man that had only just been spotted by McKay leaned around the post he was using for cover and sighted along the barrel of his rifle. "I got him."

A rifle shot cracked, but it came from high rather than low. The third gunman jerked back as if he'd been kicked in the chest. His finger tightened around his trigger, but sent its round into the street. His eyes glazed over as he dropped to his knees. Finally, he flopped forward and let out his last breath.

With one less target to worry about, McKay brought up his left hand so he could fire each of his guns at each of the gunmen. By this time, he'd backed up enough to slip around the side of the barbershop opposite from where the first gunman had ducked. From there, he could focus his aim and drive each of the other two back a few steps more.

"Circle around this asshole," the first gunman shouted.

The second man acknowledged the order with a nod and prepared himself to get moving once again. Before he could take one step toward McKay, another shot from up high drilled into the wall to the man's right. Like a loud step close to a clump of bushes, that shot flushed out the rifleman and got him running down the street.

"Wrong way!" the first gunman shouted. Before he could say anything else, a shot hissed so close to his face that the man could feel the breeze. All the color drained from the gunman's face and he ran in the opposite direction from where that last shot had landed.

After a few paces, both gunmen met up in the street. They were a few storefronts away from the barbershop and kept firing rounds toward it. The front window shattered, causing the horses inside to whinny loudly and stomp their hooves.

Sensing the tide of the fight had turned in his favor, McKay stepped into the street with both guns blazing. His lips curled back to show his gritted teeth as he fired again and again at the pair of gunmen. Those other two fired back, but were so busy trying to find a spot to hide that none of their bullets hit anything but dusty walls.

"We found ya once and we'll find ya again!" the first

gunman shouted. Despite his threat, however, he and his partner were still running in the opposite direction.

McKay held both smoking guns in steady hands as he eased down the street. His eyes glanced on all sides, but now focused on the rooftops where the gunmen had been looking during the fight. Unable to spot anything up there, McKay holstered one gun while reloading another. He reloaded the second one while running between the barbershop and its neighbor.

Moments later, he was in the saddle and putting some distance between himself and that ghost town.

THIRTY-THREE

The bank's door came open and was shut less than a heart-beat later. Kira could hear the sounds of something shifting against the floor, and held her breath while pressing herself flat against the dividing wall. She could still hear the echoes of gunshots rolling through the room, and could still feel the rumble of nearby footsteps.

Until now, she'd felt lucky that nobody had come in after her. She'd even dared to think that nobody else knew where she was. Now, as she strained to hear if anyone else was in that building with her, she wasn't feeling very lucky at all.

"Kira?" came a familiar whisper. "It's me."

She let out the breath she'd been holding and jumped to her feet. The moment she looked through the teller's window, she spotted Clint in the shadows. "Oh, my God, am I glad to see you!"

He motioned for her to keep her voice down while making his way around the dividing wall. Even though she kept herself from speaking right away, Kira thought the beating of her heart was loud enough for anyone else to hear.

"Are you all right?" Clint asked after he took a quick look at her.

Kira nodded. "What about you? I heard all the shooting. What happened out there?"

"Those three men who caught up with us on the way here managed to catch up to us again. The good news is that now there's only two of them to worry about."

"Where did they go?"

"They got out of here as fast as they could," Clint explained. "I doubt they'll be back too soon."

"If they know we're here, they could be back any minute! We've got to get out of here." As she spoke, Kira tugged against the rope that tied her to the teller's cage. The more she failed to pull free, the more frantic she got.

Clint took hold of one of her wrists and then managed to snag the other. "You need to calm down," he said as he tightened his grip to keep her from struggling.

"I can't calm down! There's men out there who want to kill me!"

"Take a breath, Kira. We won't get anywhere by flailing around like this."

Eventually, Kira eased up on her struggling. It seemed most of that was due to the hands holding her back rather than Clint's words. Either way, once she stopped struggling, Kira lost a good amount of her energy. She slumped back against the wall and slid into a seated position. Clint kept hold of her wrists and knelt down right along with her.

"Those men are after the price on your head," Clint explained.

She slowly shook her head while staring forward without seeming to see anything within the bank. "I didn't want any of this to happen. I didn't want this to go so far."

"Shooting Earl was one thing," Clint said. "But you shot at Marshal Vicker and even shot another man before you made your escape."

"What other man?"

"The one watching over Earl. The one who let you into that jail."

"I shot him?"

"I heard about it from plenty of different people, Kira. You know damn well you shot him."

"I guess I just didn't know I'd hit him." She lowered her head as the rest of her body wilted even more against the dividing wall. "I was just shooting to drive everyone back. I just wanted to get out of there, Clint. You've got to believe me."

"I do believe you," Clint replied.

Kira looked up with a bit more hope in her eyes. "You do?"

He nodded. "I did talk to plenty of folks who saw what happened. Their stories weren't exactly the same, but it seemed clear to me that you hit Ben without truly meaning to. Besides, that wound in your leg looks like you got it while you were running away and not running into a fight."

"You had a look at my wound?"

Clint chuckled and said, "I may have been preoccupied a little while ago, but I wasn't blind."

She grinned at that. "It's nothing really. I barely even knew I was hit until I was on my way out of town. If things keep up like this, the next time I get shot will probably be a whole lot worse."

"You plan on getting shot again?"

"Those men are gunning for me. You said it yourself. I've got a price on my head and even if I get turned in by you, I'm still as good as dead."

Clint got to his feet and looked through the front window. Letting out a sigh, he said, "As long as you're breathing, you're still alive."

"That's sweet, but you're not the one who's tied to this wall while gunshots are being fired a stone's throw away from you."

"True," Clint said as he tugged on the rope, loosened the knot, and pulled it over the wall. "But now, you aren't tied to that wall either."

For a moment, Kira looked like she couldn't believe her eyes. That expression became even more apparent when Clint untied her wrists. Even after the ropes were gone, she kept her arms in front of her as if they were still tied. "What's the catch?" she asked.

"No catch. I'm just banking on the fact that you're smart enough to realize I'm your best chance to get through this alive. You're unarmed, have no supplies, and are being hunted by at least two men with more on the way. There isn't much you can steal from me, and even if you did manage to get away from me, that price on your head would just keep getting bigger until every bounty hunter out there has you at the top of their list."

"And here I thought you were optimistic about all this," she said.

"I am, but we need to stick together. Also, I can do a lot more if I'm not worried about dragging you along by a rope."

Kira nodded slightly as Clint's words started to truly sink in. "And what happens if we get away from those men?"

"I take you back to Marshal Vicker. He's a good man and, from what I hear, he did his damn'dest to stop you from escaping without hurting you. He'll see to it you get what the law says you've got coming. I'd wager he'll even listen to you explain yourself, and that should go a long way in smoothing this out even faster."

"But he's the one who put a price on my head."

"You forced him into it," Clint explained. "Whether you meant to or not, you shot one man after shooting Earl. You rode out of Taloosa like one of the James Gang. What else would any marshal do after that?"

"I see your point." When she smiled at him, the familiar spark had returned to Kira's eyes. "This is so sweet of you, Clint. You really must care about me."

"I just don't like to see a bad situation get any worse."

"You care about me," she said with something of a musical tone in her voice. "Especially after . . . earlier."

"That," Clint said, "was a moment of weakness on both of our parts."

"Some parts more than others, I'd say."

Keeping his expression from cracking was difficult, but Clint managed to pull it off. "The moment I catch you trying to take advantage of this, I'll wrap you up so tightly in those ropes, you won't be able to blink."

"Fine," Kira moaned as she crossed her arms and dropped back against the dividing wall. "How much longer are we going to stay here?"

"I plan on getting some sleep," Clint said.

"What?"

But Clint had already sat down in a spot where he could see the windows and doors. His hat was pulled down and his arms were folded across his belly. Before long, Kira was curled up beside him.

THIRTY-FOUR

When the morning came, Kira was still curled up right beside Clint. He knew she wasn't going to strike out on her own with those other gunmen out there waiting for her. In fact, since those same gunmen were probably sneaking around and waiting for Kira to run, Clint figured he could take a little rest in the eye of this storm.

He'd spent most of the night half-awake, but it was one of the quietest nights he'd experienced since before he'd started riding with Ben. Before that, it had been just him and Eclipse riding across the country. The Darley Arabian might not have been a good conversationalist, but at least he gave Clint plenty of peace and quiet.

The morning light blazed into the bank, illuminating every last bit of dust that swirled through the air. Sitting there, Clint could close his eyes and hear every shutter in town knocking against its frame. He would have felt downright tranquil if he didn't know about all those gunmen out there scheming to put him down.

When he looked at her again, Clint saw that Kira's eyes were open and she was slowly getting to her feet. "I see you decided to stay," he said.

"Yeah, well . . . you made a good case for yourself last night."

"And there's plenty of time to escape once we're safely out of this town?"

For a second, Kira looked insulted. Then, she scowled and said, "Well, you sure don't seem too concerned about leaving. I figure maybe you know something I don't."

"All I know is that we can watch ourselves better in here than in the middle of the desert."

"So we're just going to live in an old bank until Marshal Vicker stumbles upon us?"

Clint stepped over to his saddlebags and took out some beans and coffee. "Nope. We're going to have a quick breakfast and ride back into Taloosa. We should be able to get there in a day or so."

"Which reminds me. Since I'm being so cooperative, I think you should split that reward with me."

"You want a piece of the bounty?" Clint asked.

"It is my head that price is on. I don't see why I shouldn't get a portion of it."

"Because," Clint replied in a colder tone of voice, "I could tie you up and bring you in whether you want to co-operate or not."

Even as she backed up a step, Kira kept her chin held high. "But you said so yourself. Things will go much easier if I cooperate."

"Maybe you forgot something. Those bounty hunters are after you, not me. Since I'm not in this for the money, letting them have you is always an option if I decide to cut and run."

She stared at him for a few seconds with her mouth hanging open. "I can't believe you said that!"

Clint shrugged.

"After all we've been through together," Kira said as she moved forward and slipped her hands along Clint's shoulders. "After all we've done together, you'd still just hand me over to a bunch of killers?"

"If you insist on making things difficult in the name of money, I would think you'd rather take your chances alone."

Her face was about an inch from Clint's. From that distance, Clint swore he could hear the thoughts running through Kira's brain like swiftly flowing water. In the blink of an eye, she dropped her sweet smile and rolled her eyes.

"Have it your way," she grumbled. "All I wanted was a bit of money to start a new life, but I guess a man's got to have his precious pay so he can buy more whiskey and gamble."

"Spare me the dramatics and get ready to ride," Clint said. "We're not about to collect any reward just yet, so let's just try to get out of this desert alive. How's that sound?"

"Do I have any choice?"

"Not really."

THIRTY-FIVE

The ghost town disappeared behind them after Clint and Kira saddled up their horses and snapped the reins. It was surprising just how quickly it disappeared. When Clint took a quick look over his shoulder, he swore that the whole place had just sunk into the sand. Of course, the glaring sun and miles of reflective sand might have had something to do with that particular illusion.

There was a good reason for traveling at night instead of when the sun was beating down upon the baked dunes. Not only did the heat feel like it could cook a man from the inside out, but the blazing light played tricks on the eyes.

Some men talked about seeing things like pools of water or even entire cities. Clint found just the opposite to be true. The raw sunlight covered more things up than anything else. Blinding white rays bouncing off a sea of sand turned nearly everything in sight into one big blur. Once the sweat started rolling into his eyes, Clint could barely make out the back of Eclipse's neck.

One positive effect of the hot sun and miles of barren wastes was that it made Kira too uncomfortable to say much along the way. She and Clint spent a good portion of their ride trying to deal with the heat and make sure they were still going in the right direction. Just when he thought those were the only problems he would have to deal with at that moment, Kira found her voice again.

"Why did we come all the way out here?" she asked.

"What?"

"If you found me so quickly, why did you take me all the way out to that ghost town just to drag me back?"

"I wanted some time to figure you out," Clint replied. "After seeing what you'd done and hearing the stories, I wanted to spend some time with you myself. Also, since Vicker would post his reward in Taloosa first, that's probably where the first batch of bounty hunters would come from. I'd rather face them out here in the open instead of on a street filled with innocent people."

"You wanted to spend time with me?" Kira asked, completely ignoring everything else Clint had said. "That's so romantic."

"I'm sure you'll understand if I don't take your idea of romance to heart."

"Say what you want about me, Clint Adams. There's a spark in your eyes when you look at me and there's no way for you to deny it."

Clint didn't waste any breath trying to deny it. He just wished there was some way he could stop feeling it.

"Is that why you're taking the long way back to town?" she asked. "Because you don't want to be rid of me so fast?"

"If there's any more bounty hunters on your trail, they'll be taking the direct route out of town. Also, this way has been clear so far, so we'll take it until we meet any resistance."

The smirk on Kira's face remained intact. "And I suppose the next thing you'll say is that we stayed in that bank the other night simply because it had the best view of the street."

"It was a difference between having to watch one door

and window or watching the entire horizon. Which would you prefer?"

"I don't know," Kira said sarcastically. "I think I would have preferred someplace that didn't have a body laying outside the front door."

Clint pulled back on his reins and turned Eclipse so he could look Kira directly in the eyes. His innards were starting to get as hot as his back, but didn't have anything to do with the unrelenting sun. "I've had just about enough of you," he said. "I'm trying to keep you alive so you can face real justice instead of a lynch mob's noose or a bounty hunter's gun, and all I get is your attitude. I try to help folks when I can, but this is one of the few times where I'm regretting it."

"We'll see how charitable you are when you're handed that reward money," she shot back. "I'll be rotting in a jail while you count up all that cash and we'll just see whose interests you have at heart."

"Maybe you're forgetting that you shot your future husband in the balls! I'd say you've got some jail time coming!"

"After the beatings he's given to me and God only knows how many other women, Earl's lucky I didn't aim a bit higher."

Clint's face froze before he could unleash his next flurry of angry words. His eyes had shifted away from Kira's face to catch sight of something else in the distance behind her.

"Get behind me, Kira," Clint said. When he saw that she wasn't moving, he added, "Don't argue with me, just do what I say. Someone's riding straight for us."

THIRTY-SIX

The moment Clint spotted the lone rider approaching, the glare from the sunlight seemed to instantly disappear. He quickly got Kira behind him and shifted around in his saddle to get another look at the rest of his surroundings.

Apart from that one man, the only thing on any side was a whole lot of sand.

"All right," Clint said to Kira before the rider was close enough to hear him, "if things get too bad, I want you to get out of here."

"Where should I go?"

"Just head that way," he said while nodding toward the east. "There was a rock formation in that direction that you should be able to pick out from a ways off. It has a small cave. You might have to ride for a while, but it's the only place I know for certain there's shelter."

"If I find some other place along the way, I'll mark it."

Clint nodded quickly. "Fine. Now just let me do the talking here and don't get riled up by anything anyone says. In fact, here." As he spoke, Clint pulled the bandanna from around Kira's neck and started to tie it over her mouth. "Just act like a prisoner. That should keep too many questions from being asked."

Although Clint wasn't certain how much the approaching man had seen, there was no use in worrying about it. For the time being, he just turned in his saddle and made sure his Colt was in plain sight. Before too much longer, the rider slowed down and came to a stop roughly seven paces from where Clint was waiting.

Nodding, Clint said, "I thought it might be you, McKay."

The bounty hunter nodded. "I see you found our girl."

"Our?"

"Sure. Since there's still plenty of gunmen out there after her, I figured you'd be more open to the offer I made."

Clint let out a quick laugh. "I wasn't the one dodging bullets in the street of that ghost town. Seems to me like you need help a hell of a lot more than I do."

McKay shifted uncomfortably in his saddle. Rolling his eyes a bit, he finally started to nod. "You got me there, but that's all the more reason why you should reconsider. I drew plenty of fire away from you. Hell, I drove them assholes out of town altogether. Without me, you two probably wouldn't have been able to get out alive."

Just when McKay's smile became arrogant, Clint brought it back down again by saying, "And if I hadn't taken my rifle onto that rooftop, you'd still be laying in that street with more holes in you than an old bucket."

"That was you up there?"

"Who'd you think it was?"

"I thought it was another one of those assholes. They nearly got me cornered without any way out."

"I saw that," Clint said patiently. "When I could tell that you didn't see it, I pitched a rock at one of the gunmen you missed."

McKay was quiet for a moment as he replayed that night in his head. When he came to that moment where he'd heard a rattle followed by a muttered curse, he grinned. "I guess I owe you my thanks."

"Think nothing of it," Clint said dryly. "Now move along."

"I got more to offer than just some cover fire," McKay continued.

"Like what?"

"Like news of where those men went after they rode out of that town. There's more of them than just those three, you know."

"Is that a fact?"

McKay nodded. "It sure is. You were smart to get out of that town, but there sure ain't nowhere to hide out here. Those men know this desert like the backs of their hands. They'll come back for you soon enough and they'll kill you if it means getting their hands on that woman. The best you can hope for is that they just take her from you and leave you alive. Either way, it won't turn out good."

"So what have you got to offer?" Clint asked. "I mean, besides cutting yourself in for a chunk of the reward money?"

"I can help you escort the lady back into Taloosa. Along the way, you'll have an extra set of eyes watching out for an ambush and an extra set of guns for when those killers decide to make their next play."

"What percentage are you asking for?"

"Forty," McKay replied. "Since I didn't go through the trouble of tracking her down, I can't rightly ask for half. But I am putting my neck on the line to bring her back."

"That seems fair, but I stay with her the whole way. That means you ride ahead and scout while I keep her in line. Since I'm the one that did all the tracking and made the capture, I think it's only fair you do the hard riding to earn your cut."

"So you'll agree to forty percent?"

"That's forty for you and sixty for me," Clint said.

Grinning, McKay stuck out his hand. "Never hurts to make sure."

"Let's just say I know how bounty hunters think."

McKay nodded. "Forty for me and sixty for you. I do the hard riding and you stay with her. After hearing about the way she treated her own husband, I can't say I'm too upset about that arrangement."

"We've got a deal," Clint said while shaking McKay's hand. "But the moment I see you're double-crossing me, I'll bury you in this desert before you know what hit you."

McKay didn't so much as flinch. "I wouldn't expect any less. I've dealt with my share of bounty hunters too."

"Perfect. I just hope your horse is well rested. You've got a whole lot of riding ahead of you."

THIRTY-SEVEN

They rode through the desert at a steady pace. Clint and Kira rode side by side, while McKay made a slow circle around them. McKay kept about a quarter of a mile between himself and the middle of the circle, which allowed him to make sure all sides were clear while the entire group moved forward.

McKay never strayed from his pattern and never stopped until Clint signaled for them to stop for a rest.

Clint liked having someone else to talk to for a change, and even swapped a few jokes with the bounty hunter whenever McKay was close enough to hear them.

Kira, on the other hand, wasn't so content with the arrangement. Even though the bandanna was back around her neck instead of over her mouth, she barely said a word throughout most of the day. There was always an intense glare aimed in Clint's direction, but she had an even more intense one for McKay whenever he rode by.

"Are you crazy?" she whispered after several hours of forced silence.

Forced or not, Clint was enjoying that silence very much and hated to hear it end. Still, he knew better than to expect a good thing to last forever. "You don't like McKay?" he asked as a way to get the ball rolling.

"No, I don't like him!" She stopped and twisted around until she spotted the bounty hunter making his rounds. Leaning in and lowering her voice, she said, "He just wants to cash in the reward and he'll do anything to get it."

"I know. He made a good offer and I took it."

"And I suppose you're just willing to trust him?"

"I watched every move he made the night when those gunmen came looking for you. First of all, I know for certain that he's not a part of whatever group it was that shot up that ghost town. He was in their sights just like we were."

"So what?"

"I also watched as he tried to get off that street without a fight."

She snorted under her breath and said, "So he's a coward on top of everything else. That's perfect."

"Only drunks and idiots run into a gunfight. McKay isn't either of those."

"All right then. I agree. Let's just trust him with our lives."

"Second," Clint went on as if Kira wasn't in the middle of her own rant, "there's no reason for McKay to be anything but up front with us. I met with him before and he offered the same deal. So far, he hasn't done anything to prove he's not trustworthy."

"Maybe he's just waiting for the best time," Kira snipped. "You ever think of that?"

"If that's the case, then I'd rather have him right here where I can keep my eye on him than out there where he's got hundreds of miles of desert to lay a trap for us."

Kira stopped short and thought that one through. Then she smiled and nodded. "I'll go along with that."

This time, Clint's voice was the one dripping with sarcasm. "Oh, good. I'm so glad the fugitive agrees with me."

"If this goes badly, then I'll be coming after you next, Clint Adams."

Before Clint could answer, he heard the familiar rhythm of McKay's horse speed up. Not only that, but it was drawing closer as well. Clint drew Eclipse to a stop and Kira did the same so they could wait for the bounty hunter to close in.

"I spotted a few riders up ahead of us," McKay said once he drew up alongside Clint.

"Are they the same ones from town?" Clint asked.

"I can't say for sure. I do know they turned and ran as soon as they knew they'd been spotted."

"Damn. That means they know which way we're headed."

"Sure," Kira said. "Or somebody pointed us out to them." The way her eyes were focused on McKay, there was no doubt who she was accusing.

The bounty hunter shrugged off her angry glare. "I'm just doing what you asked, Clint."

"I know. How long ago did you spot them?"

"I turned and came back here the minute they rode off."

"Think you could pick up their trail and find out where they went?"

McKay grinned and nodded. "Shouldn't be too hard. Their tracks should be fresh even in this damn sand."

"Then go. Find out where they went and how many of them there are. We're going to do a little backtracking and then head toward Taloosa from the north."

"Got it. Should I meet up with you somewhere or just try to pick up your tracks?"

"I'll meet you five miles east of here. If things get too bad, fire some shots in the air. I should be able to hear it from quite a ways off."

Nodding while tipping his hat, McKay brought his horse around and pointed its nose in roughly the same direction from which he'd come. He then touched his heels to the horse's sides and snapped the reins. The horse thundered away in a cloud of dust.

"Before you say a word," Clint warned as he felt Kira start to stir, "we're heading for a spot that I know is safe. It's also not too far from Taloosa."

"We could always go all the way back into town," she offered. "I'd rather take my chances there than out here. Also, I bet Marshal Vicker would lend a hand."

Clint wasn't affected in the least by the growing hope in Kira's voice. "After seeing how gun-happy those men were, I'm not about to lead them into a town that's inhabited."

She nodded, albeit slowly. "So, you still think we can trust that bounty hunter?"

"I guess we'll find out soon enough."

THIRTY-EIGHT

Making it back to that rock formation was no easy task. Unlike the first time, Clint was on a tight schedule. Ironically, trying to make his way back to those rocks was several times harder than when he'd stumbled upon them in the first place. He had a rough idea of where to go, and Kira helped out once they got closer.

"They should be over there," she said while pointing to the right of where they were headed.

Clint grumbled and looked over to her. "If I find out you knew exactly where we were going and didn't help out until now . . ."

"I planned out where I wanted to go, remember? Besides, you didn't tell me exactly where we were headed until a little while ago."

Since he began to recognize the lay of the land, Clint decided not to argue with her anymore. Doing so was just a waste of breath anyway and he didn't have much breath to spare. Both Eclipse and Kira's horse pushed themselves to their limits in crossing the desert so quickly. Clint didn't want to strain the animals so much, but they didn't have much choice now that they'd been tracked down so soon.

When the rocks finally came into sight, the sun was

about to dip beneath the horizon. Clint's goal had been to get themselves situated before dark since that would be the prime time for any ambush to occur. Even though that goal had been accomplished, Clint wasn't feeling much better.

"I want you to hide in there," Clint said as he rode up to the mouth of the small cave. "Get all the way in the back and start gathering rocks to wall yourself in."

Kira's eyes widened to the size of saucers. "You really are crazy if you think I'm doing that! I've had nightmares about being buried alive and I sure as hell aren't going to do it on my own."

"You don't need to be buried alive," Clint explained. "Just make a place to hide from anyone who comes looking for you."

"So you're going to leave me here?"

"I need to meet McKay. If there's any trouble, I don't want you to be in the middle of it. I didn't come this far to bring you in alive to lose you now."

"That's so sweet," she said with a bright smile. Her smile dropped off suddenly when she asked, "And what if McKay pulls something?"

"All the more reason for you to be somewhere else. Still, I don't think he'll try anything. He's had plenty of chances so far and hasn't done anything wrong. Bounty hunters think about money first and he stands to make a good amount of money with the deal we've struck."

"How long am I supposed to wait in there?" she asked grudgingly.

"If I'm not back by dawn, start walking back to town."

"Wait a second! Walking? I'm supposed to walk through the desert back to town?"

"You think I should trust you with a horse? Why should I believe you wouldn't just head out of here the moment I left?"

"This is great! You have an easier time trusting some bounty hunter than me?" When she saw she wasn't getting through to Clint, Kira pouted just a bit and added, "What if something happened to you? I could die out here all by myself."

Although he tried to resist, Clint felt himself breaking down. Although he knew what she was doing, he couldn't argue with the fact that she had a point. This, like so many other moments in his life, boiled down to a matter of trust.

"If you strike out on your own," Clint said, "you'd better hope you get all the luck on your side because I won't lift a finger to help."

"I understand."

"And if you do take off, I'll make it my personal mission to hunt you down again, reward or not."

She nodded with the anxiousness of someone who knew they were about to get exactly what they wanted.

Handing over the reins, Clint said, "Try to keep your horse out of sight. There should be enough room in there, but it might be tricky calming it down. Also, if anyone looks in there, you won't be able to hide yourself and a horse."

"Clint, there was no way I was walling myself up in there. You should know that."

"Yeah, I kind of figured. Just try to be safe and if I'm not back by morning, head back to town and turn yourself in. It would be better if I was there to speak for you, but that's still the best chance you've got."

"I will. And one last thing." Kira pulled Clint closer so she could plant a kiss on him that curled the toes inside his boots. Her mouth opened just enough for her tongue to slip out, and she tasted him as though she was savoring her last meal. When she eased back again, she said, "Be careful."

THIRTY-NINE

Clint met up with McKay just as the bounty hunter was starting to ride away from the spot they'd agreed upon. When he saw Clint coming, McKay stopped and rode back wearing a big smile on his face.

"I was just starting to think you'd run out on me," McKay said. "What kept you?"

"I've been a little busy. Did you catch up with those gunmen?"

"Yeah. I don't think I was spotted, but I can't be sure about that. With this much wide-open space, it's kind of hard to stay hidden."

"Where are they?"

McKay pulled in a deep breath and shook his head in disbelief. "The real question is where they aren't. From what I saw, they didn't even have a camp set up. There was one small wagon, which I think had supplies, but other than that it was just a whole lot of riders."

"How long's it been since that price was put on Kira's head?"

The bounty hunter barely even had to think about that one. "Just a few days. And as far as I know, I was the only other bounty hunter in Taloosa when the notice was posted."

Clint nodded at the way McKay answered his next question just as he'd thought it. "Even if word was put out over telegraph, that many men could never get here so quickly. That means they must have been called in some other way. There's also the possibility that they were already there and just aren't professionals.

"Those men move more like a gang of killers than bounty hunters. The way they're stomping around, they're not looking to capture anyone alive. Considering the target, I'm actually surprised that they wouldn't want to bring her in alive."

It was plain for Clint to hear the distaste in the bounty hunter's voice. McKay's words almost carried an unspoken apology for the behavior he expected out of his fellow hunters. "So if they're not bounty hunters," Clint said, "then that points to them being hired guns. And if that's the case, that leads to one big question."

"Who hired them?" McKay said, finishing Clint's line of reasoning.

"Exactly. I might be able to find out if I did some investigating back in Taloosa, but there's not enough time for that. There is another way that can be even better, but carrying it out is awfully risky."

McKay wiped away some of the sweat pouring from his forehead. "We'll need any edge we can get against that many guns." Suddenly, he started looking around in all directions. "By the way, where's Kira?"

"She's safe for now. I made sure of that personally."

"Good. Do you think she might try to get away?"

After a few seconds, Clint shook his head. "She'll think about it, but she'll change her mind once she weighs her options. She already knows she doesn't stand a chance against these gunmen and riding back into town on her own will just guarantee her the worst sentence possible.

Seeing as how that's what she was riding out to avoid in the first place, I'm wagering that she's going to stay put. At least, she will for a little while."

"I guess that's better than risking losing her altogether."

Clint could hear the earnest tone in McKay's voice and knew right then that the bounty hunter's heart was in the right place. The fact that McKay didn't even ask for details on where Kira was earned more points in Clint's book.

"So what's this risky plan of yours?" McKay asked.

FORTY

The desert was covered with an inky blackness that was similar to a thick cloud of smoke. At first, it was hard to see much of anything, but after a while, the eyes would adjust and vague shapes could be distinguished. For the men riding out on their patrol, the night wasn't anything special. Their eyes hadn't seen much of anything else, so they got around as easily as the critters scurrying from one rock to another.

They spotted McKay without much trouble and signaled to each other that the chase was on.

It took McKay a few moments to realize he was in the other men's sights, but once he did, he was off like a shot. He brought his horse around and snapped the reins while only sparing few quick glances over his shoulder.

The riders were experienced enough to know better than to start firing right away. Their guns were drawn, but they were still out of range. Even after they gained a little more ground, they still kept from pulling their triggers since they were moving too fast to expect any sort of accuracy.

Another couple of signals were passed between the two men and they split up to close in on McKay from two sides. They dug their spurs into their horses' flanks, leaned in, and hung on for their lives as the animals bolted even faster into the darkness.

McKay had his gun out as well, but could barely make out the shapes of the two men that were closing in on him. Firing his gun at them would have just been a waste of bullets. The men were gaining. He could tell that much just by the way the sound of those horses' steps grew in his ears.

Just when he thought he wasn't going to make it far enough, McKay spotted what he was looking for and steered toward it. The torch was stuck in the sand and sputtering just enough to catch his eye. After McKay passed it, he turned sharply to the left and shifted in his saddle.

McKay's .44 blazed through the darkness, sending a quick series of shots through the air. The thunder coming from the gun was almost deafening since it shattered the silence that was normally so complete in the middle of the desert.

The rider who'd been closing in on McKay's left pulled on his reins so hard that he nearly caused his horse to flop onto its side. The animal kept its footing by a slim margin and fought to regain its balance. As it went through those motions, the man on its back fired off a few shots of his own that hissed over the bounty hunter's head.

The rider who'd been closing in on McKay's right was nowhere to be seen.

A few seconds ago, the rider had been in his saddle and charging through the desert with his gun in his hand. He'd had his target in his sights and on the run, which meant all was right with the world. Then, his horse had stumbled, the rider had toppled to the ground, and had seemed to get swallowed up by the sand.

The wind had been knocked from his lungs.

His entire body ached.

He couldn't even see.

It felt as if he'd been wrapped up in a blanket and stuffed

under the ground. Suddenly, he felt something move beside him as a set of eyes appeared directly in front of him.

"Shut your mouth," Clint whispered as he could hear the rider collecting himself. When he held his Colt against the rider's head and thumbed back the hammer, Clint knew he had the man's full attention.

"That's better," Clint said.

"Wh . . . where am I? What happened?"

"You're in quite a pickle," Clint responded. "And the only way out of it is for you to answer a few quick questions."

"What the hell?"

While the rider was still off balance, Clint pressed his advantage by pressing the Colt a little harder against the rider's skull. That shut the man up and fixed his eyes solely upon Clint's face.

"How many of you are out here?" Clint asked.

"Who are—"

"How many?"

"S-six. No, wait. Seven. There's seven of us."

"All right," Clint said as he eased up on the Colt. "What are you doing out here?"

"Hey. You're that fella who was with that man that was wounded. Not the one who got his balls shot, but that other one."

"You're not answering my question."

"We're out here for that bitch who did the shooting."

"You're bounty hunters?"

Before he could think of anything else better, the rider spit out, "Not really."

"Then why go through so much trouble? Tell me now or you won't be leaving this hole."

Hearing that brought a few things into stark focus. The rider was suddenly aware of the sand and ground wrapping around him on nearly every side. He could also feel the barrel of the Colt digging into the side of his head, which sent a wave of fear and panic through his entire body.

"There's another reward being offered for her. It's more than the one offered by the law. If we bring her in, we can claim both of 'em."

"Who's offering the other reward?"

"Earl Runquist, who else?"

"I suppose he doesn't want Kira brought in alive?"

The rider let out a laugh that was more of a nervous croak. "You got that right. He says that the bitch took something from him that's worth a whole lot of money. He says he don't even want it back if'n we find it. So long as we kill her and let her know Earl sent his regards, he says we can keep the money and even claim the reward."

"He knows for a fact she took it?"

"Hell, yes! That's probably why she shot him in the first place."

"And what was she supposed to have taken?"

"Some pouch full of gold coins and a few other jewels. I don't know exactly, but Charlie says he knows Earl's speaking the truth."

"Charlie?"

"He's the one who got us together so's we could go after her," the rider said. "He and Earl go way back. I don't know anything else, mister. Please don't leave me in here anymore."

Clint eased the Colt back and moved away from the rider. As he went, he deftly swiped the pistol that had wound up lying only a few inches from the rider's hand. "You want to leave? You'll just have to do that on your own."

The next thing the rider heard was a rustle of something heavy against the sand followed by a couple footsteps. Something dropped down against the rider's face as hooves from a horse somewhere nearby thumped against the ground.

The rider's head filled with panic.

Thoughts of being buried in some shallow grave made him twitch and thrash against the ground. When he reached out to feel where he was, his hands became wrapped up in something rough that suffocated him.

He started to scream and kick. All he wanted was to sit up and run away, but his brain told him that there was nowhere he could go.

His body, on the other hand, acted on its own and simply tried what the rider was too afraid to do on his own.

He sat up.

The rough covering fell away from his head and he suddenly felt the cool desert breeze wash over his face.

"What the hell?" the rider muttered.

Looking around, he saw the pit he'd been lying in was just a small ditch that had been quickly scooped out of the sand. The covering that had wrapped him up was a smelly horse blanket that had also been covered with a thick layer of sand.

The rider shifted around and kept looking. His senses were telling him one thing, but the fear coursing through his blood was still telling him another.

Thinking back to the questions he'd been asked was like trying to remember a bad dream. He'd thought that face was familiar, but it seemed more unreal with every passing second.

"Hello?" he said to the shadows.

Nobody answered.

He could hear a few gunshots in the distance as well as what sounded like a familiar voice. The rider nearly jumped from his skin when he heard something move no more than a few feet away. When he twitched to get a look, he saw his own horse standing there, waiting patiently.

In the distance, another horse was racing past a small torch sticking out of the ground.

FORTY-ONE

"Where on earth did you learn that trick?" McKay asked once Clint had caught up to him.

Clint was still wearing the same grin that had been on his face after he'd rolled out from under the covered ditch. "It's sort of an old Indian trick, but I put my own twist on it."

"I'll have to remember that one. Did it work?"

"Oh, yeah. There's about seven of them in that man's group, but there could be more. Earl sent them."

Shaking his head, McKay said, "I knew they couldn't all be bounty hunters."

"They were promised a reward other than the one on that notice. The man I talked to made it sound like a small fortune. You know anything about that?"

After thinking it over for a bit, McKay shook his head once more. "I only know about the price that Marshal Vicker put on her head, but I didn't talk to Earl about it. He could very well be offering that added incentive as a way to make certain that lady winds up six feet under. Can't say as that's much of a surprise."

"What about the rider that was following you?" Clint asked. "Did you shake him?"

"Once he emptied his gun and realized he didn't have his partner with him any longer, he turned tail and headed back."

"Good work."

"This worked out real well, but you know it's just gonna light a fire under the rest of those gunmen. If they are after a heap of money on top of that reward, they'll be getting itchy trigger fingers right about now."

"Sounds like you may be speaking from experience," Clint pointed out.

"I sure am. Cashing in bounties is one thing. If the reward gets too big and is paid under the table, it gets way too easy for men to justify killing before anything else. Those are the sorts of jobs I steer away from. They're too damn messy."

"You want to back out of this job? I wouldn't blame you."

McKay didn't hesitate before saying, "Nah. I already came this far. Besides, you need all the help you can get. That is, unless you had horse blankets buried around this desert intended for the rest of those men."

"Not exactly, but I do think we can wrap this up without too much more fuss."

As he spoke, Clint took the spyglass from his saddlebag. He placed it to one eye while keeping the other one open. That way, he could see more than just a magnified patch of black. After a bit of searching, he found the flickering torch.

"Is he still there?" McKay asked.

"Yep. He's just getting up and realizing what happened to him. He's kicking at the blanket. Oh . . . he's mad."

McKay laughed. "I'll bet he is. You didn't leave him with his gun, did you?"

"I got the one he was holding when his horse got tripped up by that other ditch I dug. He might have another one on him. Tell you the truth, I probably wanted to get the hell out from under that blanket worse than he did."

Clint watched as the stunned rider filled his lungs with fresh air and got his bearings back. Before too long, the rider was climbing back into the saddle.

"He's about to get moving," Clint reported as he lowered the spyglass.

"Then it shouldn't be long before he stirs up that trouble I was warning you about."

"And that's the best way to get all those men in one place. From there, we should be able to put an end to this once and for all."

McKay cleared his throat and shifted uncomfortably in his saddle. "That's what I wanted to talk about. I enjoy working with you and all, but this seems to be a bit more work than forty percent would call for."

"You're trying to squeeze me for more money? Now?"

"Better now than when it's too late and when the lead starts to fly."

Clint leaned in to get a closer look at McKay's eyes. To the other man's credit, McKay didn't so much as flinch. "You know something? I would have doubted you were a real bounty hunter unless you brought that up."

McKay smirked and shrugged his shoulders. "Business is business."

"That's right. You're in for half the money. Depending on how things turn out, maybe more."

Nodding at first, McKay reached out to offer Clint his hand. "No hard feelings, friend. I've been double-crossed too many times. It tends to make a man jumpy."

"I know just how you feel."

FORTY-TWO

Kira sat on the ledge of the rock formation with her legs dangling over the side. Her heels were only a few feet from the ground, but when she leaned back and closed her eyes, she could imagine that she was sitting on the edge of a canyon. Imagining the view from hundreds of feet up made her muscles relax and all of her troubles glide away.

That tranquility lasted for another second or two before she heard the rumble of approaching horses. Her eyes snapped open and she gripped onto the edge of the rock tight enough to turn her knuckles white. Kira didn't realize she was holding her breath until her heart began to twist in her chest and her blood started to chill.

When she finally refilled her lungs, she did so with a gasp. There was definitely someone coming, and it was too early for it to be Clint. Reflexively, she reached for her belt, but the gun wasn't there. She then slid forward and landed in front of the cave. A bit of pain from the little wound in her leg made her wince but was quickly forgotten. She didn't even limp when she ran over to her horse and quickly pulled on one of the saddle straps.

"It's all right," she said to the animal. "Just me. I'm just fixing that little itch in your side."

As she said that, Kira reached under one of the straps that crossed the horse's belly until she found a small leather bundle. Kira grinned and removed the bundle. It closed with a single flap, which she unsnapped and opened. Inside, there was a two-shot derringer.

Her victory was short-lived, however, since she could now make out the shape of the horseman coming her way. She didn't have to see in the dark to know that whoever was on that horse was armed with something that held more than two shots. That person was probably much more experienced with a gun than she was.

Kira gripped the derringer and planted her feet. For a moment, it seemed as though she was going to stand there and wait for the horseman to arrive. Then, she was overtaken by a bout of common sense and knew she needed to figure out another plan.

"Damn," she whispered while frantically looking around. The more she looked for something that would be of any help, the less she saw.

"Dammit."

She was hopping from one foot to the other by this time. Although she knew the horseman couldn't have seen her yet in the dark, that would only last until the horse got a little closer. Suddenly, she realized that the horseman might not even be headed for her. Kira squinted into the shadows and watched as the figure grew larger as it drew closer. It was coming straight for the rocks.

"Damn!"

Every part of her wanted to move. She could start running, but that would only draw attention to herself as she raced off into the desert. She could get on her horse, but that would only buy her another minute or two before she was run down or shot from her saddle. She could climb back onto the rock and shoot the horseman when he got closer, but she'd practiced with the derringer enough to know she could only hit anything if it was about ten feet in front of her and that was in broad daylight.

The horse was coming her was in a rush and that left her precious little time. If she was going to do anything besides stand there and hope for the best, she was going to have to do it quickly. Reluctantly, Kira's eyes drifted to the opening of the cave. The longer she looked at it, the smaller it seemed to get.

"Damn."

With that word still echoing in her mind, she scrambled into the cave and crawled all the way to the back. She froze in her spot when she remembered her horse was still outside. It was too late to save the horse, she decided. Whoever was coming had at least seen that horse.

"Sorry about that," she said toward the cave's opening. "You should be just fine out there."

As she talked, Kira pulled in some of the rocks that she'd gathered when Clint left. Unfortunately, she'd approached that job the way a lazy kid might approach a hated chore. She did it while Clint was looking, but her efforts had tapered off real quickly once Clint was gone. Now, she was regretting that particular decision.

She scraped up her side and gave herself a nice collection of bumps and bruises as she stacked the rocks on top of each other. Since there were only enough to form a barrier that was about a foot high, Kira lay on her side, pressed herself against the floor as best she could, and closed her eyes.

If that rider was going to lean in and start shooting into the cave, she didn't want to see it coming.

The other horse came to a skidding stop outside and a pair of heavy boots slammed down to the ground. The man outside stomped around for a few seconds before making his way into the cave. He lingered there for a bit as Kira held her breath.

Those seconds dragged by until Kira thought she was going to pass out. She tightened her grip on the derringer, while planning how she might make her final stand.

Kira's horse let out a few huffs and shifted on its hooves as the man outside walked around some more. It sounded as if the man was rummaging through something before walking back toward the cave. Once there, he leaned forward and said, "Kira, you in there?"

She let out her breath and sat up, immediately knocking her head against the top of the cave. "Jesus, Clint," she said as she crawled toward the opening. "With all the hiding and lurking we've been doing, you'd think I'd recognize you just by your footsteps."

When she emerged from the cave, she was wearing a smile. That smile dropped away when she saw the look on Clint's face.

"What's wrong?" she asked.

"What did you take from Earl?"

"Clint, what's the matter?"

"Answer my question," Clint demanded. "What did you take from Earl?"

"I took away the part of him that made him such a vicious bastard. At least, I took away enough for him to think twice before he—"

"Not that. You stole something from him. What was it?"

"I don't know what you're talking about."

Slowly, Clint nodded and his expression softened. "Sorry about that. I just heard some bad news." Opening his arms, he asked, "Are you all right?"

Kira jumped on the opportunity to pout a bit and start rubbing her head while walking straight into Clint's arms. "I hid in there just like you said, but I hurt my head when you . . . What are you doing?"

Once Kira was leaning against him, Clint moved his hands up and down along her back and sides. "I already went through your saddlebags," he said while holding her out to arm's length. "So that means you must have it on you."

"This is ridiculous!" she said while trying to get away from him. "Stop it! I told you everything."

Just as she said that, Clint's hand brushed against a spot on the front of her waist that was just off center. He pulled her shirt out of the way and snatched something that had been wedged under her belt. Holding up the pouch, Clint said, "Everything, huh?"

"I can explain that."

FORTY-THREE

"Go on," Clint said. "I'm waiting for your explanation."

"I needed some money if I was going to run away. At first, I thought I would be able to get away clean after shooting Earl. Everyone knows that Marshal Vicker is the only lawman and he was at the Armadillo. The door was unlocked just like I knew it would be, but . . .".

"But you didn't plan on Ben being there," Clint finished.

Slowly, Kira nodded. "He was there and I thought I should just turn around and walk away. But I knew I wouldn't be able to get the nerve to go back, which means Earl would just keep on doing what he does and would probably even get worse.

"I didn't think I'd be shooting my way out of that jail or out of that town," she explained. "I thought I would fire one shot and get out without any trouble. Earl's been locked up before and he's paid for whores to . . . visit him while he was in there."

"So you didn't expect anyone to be there," Clint said in a rush. "That still doesn't tell me what you took."

"I barely made it out of town. I was just firing over my shoulder and waiting for Marshal Vicker to put a bullet in my back. Everyone knows he's a dead aim and I thought

171

for certain I was going to die right then and there. When I made it out, I just kept riding.

"Then I realized I barely had any clothes and only a dollar or two in my pocket. I came back to get what I needed." Glancing up using just her eyes, Kira saw Clint was glaring back at her expectantly. "Earl had a nest egg under the floorboards, so I took that as well. I figured it would be enough for me to start over again somewhere else."

Still holding the pouch, Clint opened it and looked inside. His eyes immediately widened as he dipped a few fingers into it. When his fingers emerged from the pouch, they were holding a small gold nugget and a wad of hundred-dollar bills.

"There's more gold in here," Clint said. "As well as some more bills. Jesus, is that a diamond?"

Kira nodded.

"Where did this come from?"

After fidgeting for a bit, Kira replied, "Remember that bank we slept in?"

"Don't try to tell me it came from there."

"That's what Earl told me. He says he knew the men that broke that safe open and took what was inside."

"So that bank was abandoned with a fortune just left behind in the safe?"

"No," Kira groaned. "I don't think so. Earl told me the bank was robbed as folks were picking up and leaving that town. I didn't really care where it came from or if he was lying. All I know is that Earl knew some dangerous men and he had all this money to show for it. Why do you think I stayed with him through all the hard times?"

Clint couldn't help but laugh. "You're a real beaut, you know that?"

"Are you mad at me?"

"Does it matter?"

"We can split the money," she offered with a smile. "I'll

need it if I'm going to start over again. I mean, after I serve my jail time and all."

Shaking his head, Clint turned around as if he was just going to walk back to where Eclipse was waiting. When he turned back to face her, he'd already tucked the money and pouch into his own pockets. "This money isn't yours. You stole it."

"Earl's friends stole it. Probably. Anyway, he said he'd split it with me once we were married."

"This could be collected from any number of jobs and stored in that bank after it was deserted. It could be some-one else's nest egg. It could have come from anywhere, for all you know. The only thing that's for certain is you snuck in and made off with it."

"I took it from my own house!" Kira said defiantly. "It's mine!"

"Yeah? Well, now it's mine." Saying that, Clint turned to get some things from Eclipse's saddle.

"To hell with that, Clint Adams! You hand that over."

"There's still those killers out there, Kira. If you were smart, you'd stay on my good side until they were taken care of."

She stopped short and flashed him a cute smile. "Oh, that's right. Sorry. Please don't be mad at me."

But Clint shook his head and carried a length of rope back toward her. A few minutes later, he was riding away and Kira was wrapped up like a Christmas present inside the cave.

"What if they find me in here?" she shouted. "I can't even run or defend myself!"

Shouting over his shoulder, Clint said, "Then I suggest you shut up and pray nothing happens to me."

FORTY-FOUR

Clint rode for just a few minutes before he could see the other riders closing in on him. They appeared on the dark horizon like blackbirds lining up on a fence. His eyes were so used to the dark by this point that he could almost count them down to the last man.

Rather than steer away from the riders, Clint headed straight for them. Part of him was worried that the gunmen had been pointed in his direction and were so close to finding Kira. Another part of him wondered how the hell he and McKay had held them off this long. He decided it was the last bit of proof that those men were local gunhands instead of bounty hunters.

In a strange way, that was a nice piece of luck.

But Clint didn't have time to ponder his luck. He barely had enough time to make himself seen before the gunmen simply started taking shots at him. Suddenly, another rider bolted toward him from the left. Clint's first instinct was to draw his Colt, but he saw that it was McKay who was heading for him.

"Sorry about this," McKay said. "I tried to keep them busy, but they all headed off in this direction instead of bothering with me."

"One of them must have followed me," Clint said. "It was bound to happen sooner or later. I guess this is the proper time for it." With that, Clint pulled back on his reins and slowed Eclipse to a walk.

McKay did the same, but looked at Clint with anxious eyes. "What the hell are you doing?"

"Making a stand."

"Against all of them at once?"

"I'm sick of playing hide-and-seek out here," Clint said disgustedly. "These boys are hotheaded and greedy. They're also amateurs, which will make them sloppy. You can leave if you want."

Clint thought McKay was going to ask where he could find Kira. Instead, the bounty hunter pulled in a breath and nodded. "I think you're right. The fact we've gotten as far as we have against these assholes says they aren't that organized." He drew both guns and asked, "You want the bunch on the left or the bunch on the right?"

"Put those guns down," Clint said. "Just follow my lead and be ready to draw again if things take a turn for the worse."

"All right."

Both men swung down from their saddles and stood with their hands at their sides. The riders thundered up to them like a noisy wave before they got the signal from their leader to slow down. By the time the dust settled and the riders came to a stop, Clint counted eight men. One of the men at the middle of the group eased his horse a few more steps ahead.

"Who's Charlie?" Clint shouted.

Just as he'd hoped, that question ruffled a few feathers in the group. Clint was simply spitting out the only name he'd gotten from the man he'd questioned, but it made him look like he already had the group scouted out.

The rider who'd come forward wasn't as impressed. "That'd be me. Who the hell are you?"

"I'm tired of this desert," Clint said. "That's who."

Charlie was a burly man with wide shoulders and a muscular frame. Thick stubble coated his chin and cheeks and even in the dark, it was obvious that sand was sticking to every inch of him. "I thought I recognized you," Charlie said. "Now why the hell did you attack my men?"

"We're after the same woman," Clint explained. "It was an honest mistake."

"Tell me where she is and I might let you crawl back to Taloosa." When Charlie said that, all the men behind him drew their weapons and aimed them at Clint and McKay. "Otherwise, we can drop you both right here and find her on our own. It don't matter to me."

"I've got a better idea," Clint said. "How about we just wrap this up now?" Slowly, Clint eased his hand into his pocket. He could feel the other men tensing as they leaned forward and started to tighten their fingers around their triggers.

With a signal from Charlie, most of the other riders eased up a bit. At any rate, Clint was allowed to take the pouch from his pocket with his left hand. "I think this is what you're after," he said.

Everyone, including McKay, seemed startled to hear Clint say that.

"What you got there?" Charlie asked.

"I took it from that woman I found. I believe it's what got all you boys out here in the middle of the night."

"He's got the money!" one of the other men shouted.

Charlie leaned back and barked, "Shut up, back there!"

"But he says he took it from the woman."

"They're the ones that've been giving us all the trouble," another rider said. "Kill them both. That bitch can't be far from here."

"Goddammit, I said shut up!" Charlie roared.

But a faction of the riders had already made up their minds. Clint saw at least three or four of the men raising their guns and taking aim. Although every one of his instincts screamed for him to draw his Colt, Clint held off.

One of the riders fired his rifle, causing another of the jumpy ones to pull the trigger of his own pistol. Sparks flew, illuminating the angry looks on some gunmen's faces and the surprise that was showing on others'.

Clint stood his ground as the lead hissed through the air around him. Rather than wait for the gunmen to improve their aim, he plucked the Colt from its holster and pointed it at the closest gunman as if he was simply pointing his finger. The Colt barked and sent a bullet into the middle of that gunman's chest.

McKay had dropped to one knee while putting a .44 in his right hand. He was only a few paces from one of the overeager gunmen as well, and killed him with a shot to the head. When McKay stood back up again, he had both guns in hand and was firing into the row of gunmen.

"Stop this!" Charlie shouted as he waved his pistol at his own men. "Goddammit, listen to me!"

Clint saw one of the gunmen drawing a bead on him, and sent him to hell with a quick shot to the eye. The incoming bullets were getting closer as the gunmen were working their way up toward Clint and McKay. Just as Clint knocked another gunman from his saddle, he saw Charlie turn and fire a shot behind him.

The rest of the men were stunned and looked at Charlie as if he'd started breathing fire. A few of the men were caught in the middle of aiming at Clint and McKay, while some didn't know where to aim. All of them were now waiting to see what Charlie would do.

Keeping his gun aimed at the troublemakers in his group, Charlie glanced to Clint and said, "if you got a real offer to make, you make it right now."

Clint's Colt didn't waver from its target as he tossed the pouch through the air with his free hand.

Charlie caught it and quickly forced it open so he could

look inside. The moment he caught a glimpse of the pouch's contents, he let out a whistle. "Holy shit. You weren't joking."

"No, I wasn't. As far as I know, that's been stolen so many times from so many people it doesn't belong to anyone anymore. You take that and we'll take Kira. That way, we can both head home."

Charlie's eyes narrowed. "We came for the bitch too."

Squaring their shoulders, Clint and McKay stared right along the barrels of their guns.

"If you want to go for all of it," Clint said, "be my guest."

Charlie looked at Clint and McKay and then glanced around at what was left of his men. "Come on, boys," he said. "We got enough in here to buy us each a redhead."

Both factions backed away cautiously. Clint and McKay didn't allow themselves to take a breath until the remaining horsemen had disappeared into the night.

FORTY-FIVE

Clint and McKay rode into Taloosa with Kira riding between them. All three of them had their dusters buttoned up and their hats pulled down low so they looked fairly similar from a distance. Since they'd had nobody dogging their tails on the way home, they'd made it back after a fairly easy ride. Now, the tension was pouring from Kira like sweat from her brow.

Despite everything that happened, Clint was the first to reach out and pat her on the shoulder as they came to a stop in front of Marshal Vicker's office.

"You men here about the bounty?" Vicker asked as he stepped out of his office. It was early in the morning and he was still too bleary-eyed to take much notice of the trio before him.

Clint tipped his hat back and said, "We sure are. I think we'd like to cash it in."

Vicker's eyes widened and he exchanged a quick series of greetings with Clint and McKay. When he looked at Kira, the disappointment was clear to see on Vicker's face.

"You're damn lucky that man's doing all right," Vicker said as he nodded behind him.

Ben walked slowly from the office, keeping one hand clasped to his stomach. "Good to see you, Clint."

"How's the wound?" Clint asked.

"Better. I've even been working for the marshal some more."

That's when Clint spotted the deputy badge pinned to Ben's shirt. "Good for you, Ben."

"It'll do for a while."

Vicker helped Kira down from her saddle since her hands were still tied. "There's a cell waiting for you and a judge is on his way. I wish to hell none of this had to happen."

"She came along on her own accord," Clint said. "I can tell you all about it."

"Save it for the judge," Vicker said. "He'll be here in a few days. Now just let me get her situated, and I'll tend to that reward money."

After the marshal took Kira away, Ben gave Clint a wave so he could do his part in showing the prisoner to her new accommodations. That just left Clint and McKay in front of the office.

"Are we still splitting the money?" McKay asked.

"You did more than your part with Charlie and his boys," Clint replied. "Things wouldn't have turned out so well if I was on my own."

"I could say the same thing. Let's call it even."

"No. I promised you more if it was called for and I think it is. Here," Clint said as he dug into his pocket. "That should make up for all the sand in your boots."

McKay was just quick enough to catch what Clint had tossed to him. He could scarcely believe his eyes when he saw the wad of hundreds in his hand. "This from that pouch you handed over to Charlie?"

Clint nodded. "There was more than enough to go around."

After tucking the money away, McKay tipped his hat.

"Guess I'll be looking for a room. How about I buy the first round of drinks at the Armadillo?"

"Sounds good. After that, we'll see how much of that money I can win back from you at cards." After McKay left, Clint's smile quickly faded. He was tired, hungry, and dirty. Things had turned out as well as he could have hoped, but there was still one loose end that itched like a tick under his pants leg.

Earl lay in his bed, which was set up in its own room in Doc Cosgrove's practice. The new deputy or Vicker was normally posted outside the door, but they weren't too concerned about Earl getting up and leaving. That worked out just fine, since Earl was still planning on enjoying himself right up until his own trial.

There was a knock as the door eased open, allowing a familiar face to peek inside.

"Is there a sick little boy in here?" Lillian asked as she walked into the room.

Earl grinned and tried to sit up, but only felt a pinch between his legs that made him sit back down again. "I asked for a beauty to be sent over, but I didn't think you'd show."

She shrugged and slipped out of her wrap. "Things get rough in my line of work. Nothing personal."

"Good," Earl grunted. "I arranged to have one woman buried, so I'd hate to have you join her."

Lillian shrugged off the vague threat even quicker than she shrugged off her clothes. Standing in front of him, she propped one foot against his bed while sliding her hands along the front of her naked body. "Is that what you wanted to see?" she purred.

Nodding, Earl licked his lips and shifted uncomfortably.

Lillian's hands massaged the insides of her thighs as she slowly eased open the lips of her pussy. She spread her legs a bit more, slipped one finger inside, and then moved the other hand up to her breast.

"Let me do it," Earl grunted as he stuck out an eager hand.

Lillian pushed him back with her upper hand while still working her finger in and out of her. "Not so rough now," she said. "Or I'll have to leave."

"Shut the fuck up and let me touch that pussy. I paid for it, goddamn you."

"You paid to watch. Since you're not able to do any more, just sit back and watch."

Earl bared his teeth and snarled as he lunged forward. Pain and anger mixed on his face as he clawed for Lillian's naked body like he meant to tear a piece right off of her. "You goddamn whore! Get closer or I'll fuck you with the barrel of a shotgun! You hear me?"

Slipping another finger inside herself, Lillian dropped her free hand to the leg that was propped on the edge of the bed. She reached for the garter belt wrapped around that leg and removed the derringer she kept there.

Before Earl could utter one more contemptuous word, the derringer spit a single round into his skull.

Lillian tucked the gun away, pulled on her clothes, and walked out.

Watch for

THE IMPOSTER

296th novel in the exciting GUNSMITH series
from Jove

Coming in August!

J. R. ROBERTS

THE GUNSMITH

GIANT ACTION! GIANT ADVENTURE!

THE GUNSMITH

GIANT

GIANT WESTERNS FEATURING THE GUNSMITH

THE GHOST OF BILLY THE KID
0-515-13622-0

LITTLE SURESHOT AND THE
WILD WEST SHOW
0-515-13851-7

DEAD WEIGHT
0-515-14028-7

AVAILABLE WHEREVER BOOKS ARE SOLD OR AT
PENGUIN.COM

J799

LONGARM

**Explore the exciting Old West with one
of the men who made it wild!**

GIANT-SIZED ADVENTURE FROM AVENGING ANGEL LONGARM.

LONGARM AND THE UNDERCOVER MOUNTIE
0-515-14017-1

THIS ALL-NEW, GIANT-SIZED ADVENTURE IN THE POPULAR ALL-ACTION SERIES PUTS THE "WILD" BACK IN THE WILD WEST.

U.S. MARSHAL CUSTIS LONG AND ROYAL CANADIAN MOUNTIE SEARGEANT FOSTER HAVE AN EVIL TOWN TO CLEAN UP—WHERE OUTLAWS INDULGE THEIR WICKED WAYS. BUT FIRST, THEY'LL HAVE TO STAY AHEAD OF THE MEANEST VIGILANTE COMMITTEE ANYBODY EVER RAN FROM.